UNDER
THE SUN

REDEMPTION GRAY SERIES

REVISED & EXPANDED

BOOK 1 OF 3

"Think! Don't die."

UNDER THE SUN

REDEMPTION GRAY SERIES

REVISED & EXPANDED
BOOK 1 OF 3

S. WESTLEY KING

REDEMPTION
PRESS

Published by Redemption Press, PO Box 427, Enumclaw, WA 98022.

Toll-Free (844) 2REDEEM (273-3336)

Redemption Press is honored to present this title in partnership with the author. The views expressed or implied in this work are those of the author. Redemption Press provides our imprint seal representing design excellence, creative content, and high quality production.

Scripture used on pages 98-99 are from the New American Standard Bible®, Copyright © 1960, 1971, 1977, 1995 by The Lockman Foundation. All rights reserved.

Scripture used on page 192 is from the Holy Bible, New International Version®, NIV® Copyright ©1973, 1978, 1984, 2011 by Biblica, Inc.® Used by permission. All rights reserved worldwide.

Lyrics from "It Is Well," written by Kristene DiMarco, © 2013 Bethel Music Publishing (ASCAP), are used by permission. All rights reserved.

Classic literature is deliberately misquoted by the author, to fit the storytelling.

Text of the *Consolation of Philosophy* by Boethius is from an unknown source, though thorough research was done to try to locate the origin of it.

ISBN: 978-1-64645-374-0 (Paperback)
978-1-64645-376-4 (ePub)
978-1-64645-375-7 (Mobi)

LCCN: 2021903101

CHAPTER 1

UNDER THE SUN:
SETTING THE STAGE

"**Y**OU CAN'T FIND HAPPINESS UNDER a rock in Montana," my teacher told me. Until now, it's the only place I ever really have.

I know I'm going to have to do some explaining when I get home, but I'm not sure I know how to put any of it into words. I threw my phone out the window in Nebraska, so I don't have any pictures, and I'm not sure what good they would do anyway. I guess I'll make use of this empty English notebook and try to recreate the past few days. Maybe then it'll make sense.

Those few days ago—along with the city, concrete, smog, and school drama—are now 1,500 miles behind me as I sit on a park bench by a river as wide and flowing as the highway near my house back in Texas. The sun is setting here in Livingston, Montana, and the wind carries my thoughts over the dandelions in their various stages of life. I've been sitting here for hours, just watching the shadows from the trees stretch across the scene as I try to understand what just happened to me.

In the past three days, I've driven through six states, seen the Great Plains, the Black Hills, and made it to the mountains of Montana. But I don't feel like a tourist. More like an explorer—not to settle, but to discover. And I have. But I don't know what to make of it. I feel like a new person, like I died, yet am alive for the first time. Like I've been emptied but remain filled. Like I've been set free but am bound to something new. Truth. But what is it?

CHAPTER 2

FRIDAY MORNING: THE SHOW JUST GOES ON

7:15 a.m.

ONLY A FEW MORE FRIDAYS before graduation. On my way to school, I pay particular attention to the things I won't miss. I won't miss the busy intersection where the crosswalk is just a place for turning cars to honk at me. I won't miss the hill sloping toward school that is just smooth enough to skate down . . . and just rugged enough to spit up pebbles big enough to put Newton's first law of motion into effect. I won't miss hiding my skateboard behind the gym so the jocks won't think I'm a skater and the skaters won't think I'm a poser. I won't miss the squawking of the popular boys trying to impress the popular girls, or the chirping of the popular girls trying to impress each other. I won't miss the dread I feel every morning going toward the windowless building with security guards at every door and being corralled between hourly bells to sit and be talked at.

7:29 a.m.

I will miss my tree. I don't even know what kind of tree it is. Does anyone even know the names of trees anymore? Anyway, it was my tree. Every day since I first climbed it my freshman year, that tree has been my secret morning home, a buffer zone between the time I show up and the time the minute bell rings. At first, I thought maybe I could watch from the tree toward the wide concrete steps leading to the narrow glass doors and catch on to the norms and rules of teenage interaction. Well, I never did figure it all out or my place in it, but I have come to appreciate the daily dramatic entertainment the stage of the steps supplied.

7:42 a.m.

Today is not much different than any other day, except it's the first day without my granddad. Sitting in my tree, I pull from my backpack his journal that I stole. I can't tell whether I'm studying the worn black cover or if it is studying me. The heavy presence of his absence is interrupted by a commotion down by the steps. I quickly shove the journal deep in my backpack and zip it tight.

Last week, the theater department did their big play, *West Side Story*. Today it's not in the auditorium; it's a real-life interpretation. Two Latino gangs come face to face. I imagine them snapping their fingers to the beat as the clans approach. No, wait. It's the Trojan War. Two greats meet face to face, and I'm sure a woman is their battle. Their heads move side to side as they bump chests. They look like puffed-up grackles squawking over the last crumb of a spilled bag of chips.

Antsy for some action, opposing crowds pull out their phones and cheer for mutual destruction. The heavyset one with the thin, stereotyped mustache gives the skinny one with something to prove a slight push. Not backing down, the under-dog swings a few wild punches. He should have listened to his mom's advice instead of hanging with this crowd egging him on. I get a better look and suddenly recognize Angel, a kid I used to hang out with in elementary school. I haven't seen him since. The playground was a different world back then.

The big guy somehow grabs a wildly slung arm and gives it a twist and downward thrust. Even from my vantage point, I almost hear it snap. Scream-ing in pain, Angel gets no sympathy from his flee-ing crew or the rent-a-cops that come trotting on scene, almost as comedic relief. I don't know what would be worse, having a dislocated elbow forced into handcuffs or being abandoned by the friends you put all your value into. I can't imagine it being both.

The bell rings, and kids rush like curtains over the set and actors.

I come down from my tree and join the ruffling crowd. As I pass, I try to make eye contact with

Angel, who's being guided away still screaming in pain, but he's too caught up in his moment in the spotlight to notice. I wonder where his life is headed. I wonder about mine. At least he took a stand. At least he did something. I've just been watching life pass by like a bad show, commercials and all.

8:02 a.m.

Walking into English class, I pull out my notebooks and class copy of *Catcher in the Rye*, the worst book I've ever read. To be fair, it's one of the only books required by high school English that I have read (either because it was the shortest book we've had to read or because Mr. Adams said it was the "last great American novel"—that also happened to be the shortest book we've had to read).

Mr. Adams is possibly the most positive person you could ever imagine. He loves every book he reads, tries to find the positive in every day, and forces that mindset on everyone who walks into his classroom. After writing an inspirational quote on the board, Mr. Adams starts every day with "It's a beautiful day." Then he randomly draws popsicle sticks with our names on them out of a coffee can and asks, "What are you most thankful for today?"

Every day, my faith is put to the test as I pray he won't pick my name. Like every day, I sit like a dead rock hiding under concrete and soil, as if lack of spirit would qualify me for exemption from participation. But today I sit deeper, deader, and don't even feel like I have a spirit to lack.

"Redemption Gray, what are you most thankful for today?" *Of all days, why today?*

"I'm thankful we're almost done talking about *Catcher in the Rye*," I retort honestly and with an unintentionally mean spirit. The honest answer is a mistake.

"Oh, Redemption! But it captures a generational psyche of American youth." *Why did I engage?* He takes it further. "What about it are you thankful to be done with?"

"He's whiny, he's immature, and it would have probably been a better story if he would have died at the end."

"What if you were Holden? Would you wish yourself that same fate?"

"If it saves a generation from reading about it, yes."

"What are you so unhappy about, Redemption?" Mr. Adams knows I hate being called Redemption, and he knows I don't want to participate. What's he going to do, fix me in front of everyone? Save me? Does he really want to know?

Words just come out. "What's happiness got to do with it?"

"If you haven't found it, you won't find it in anything," he counsels. "If you *have* found it, you'll find it in everything."

I hate feeling small, but that's how it seems the Prophet of Positive Thinking secures his power. He continues talking, but I am shutting him out, until—"you can't find happiness under a rock in Montana."

Mr. Adams talking, the desks, walls, and the other students all seem to evaporate, creating a fog around my attention. That phrase becomes the only thing that seems to exist as the classroom fades.

You can't find happiness under a rock in Montana.

8:18 a.m.

To break the haze, I get up and walk down my aisle, in front of Mr. Adams, and toward the door. I grab the restroom pass (a hubcap painted yellow with a smiley face) from a hook on the wall and walk out of the class into the hall.

Taking a deep breath, I analyze whether I really need to go to the restroom. I head to my tree to think instead. Before I get there, a subconscious jingle of my dad's extra car keys in my backpack's side pocket makes me realize I walked out of class with all my stuff. I follow my feet around to the teachers' parking lot and click the unlock button until I locate the beep of my dad's car.

CHAPTER 3

FRIDAY MORNING: EXIT STAGE NORTH

8:25 a.m.

Leaning against the trunk of my dad's car as the gas tank fills up, I take another deep breath and find myself thinking about the bird I had a year ago. My own voice replays in my mind: "You left the cage door open!" I don't know why I tried blaming Mom and Dad. I knew it was me. I had that bird for almost year . . . but I'm surprised it stayed alive that long. What a miserable life it had. I rarely fed it or cleaned its cage, much less gave it attention and a sense of purpose. No wonder it flew away.

The sun is still separating itself from the sky-scraper horizon and stretching into the feathered gray-blue sky. I can feel the adrenaline pumping through my body, exhilarating my legs and arms. Telephone wires and traffic lights. A high-speed crowd of racing cars.

I am surprised there are no birds in the sky and instantly hate myself for wondering where they are. I can hear Mr. Adams emphasizing and reemphasizing the thoughts of Holden Caufield— "Where do the ducks go in winter? Where do the ducks go in winter?"—as if it had meaning. Maybe that's what I didn't like about the book. Maybe the book was okay without Mr. Adams insisting there was deep meaning in every sentence, every object, and every scene.

The gas pump clicks. I get in the car, put "Montana" in my phone for directions, pop the tab of a Red Bull, and hit play on my high-energy playlist. I am ready to chase the wind.

Accidentally peeling out into traffic, I screech the tires again by slamming on the brakes. Stoplight number one. Then—I'm on the road.

8:34 a.m.

Stoplight number two. Three. Eight. Have there always been this many stoplights between the school and the highway? Have I ever caught that many red lights in one drive? Is it an omen? No. There isn't meaning in everything. It's just city traffic. It's why good people cuss.

By the time I'm circling around the on-ramp to the highway, my hands are already cramping from clenching the wheel. For the first time in my driving life, I push the pedal to the metal, feeling another rush of excitement and fear as a little car entering the three-lane world of big trucks and professional speeders.

9:15 a.m.

As the jarring survival mode of getting on a vaguely familiar highway in the middle of the metroplex balances with the steady flow of traffic and a better sense of general direction, I start to feel like I belong on the road. Like I'm finally going somewhere.

Where are all these other people going? What are their stories?

Within a cluster of cars, trucks, and semis going roughly the same speed, I can't help but appreciate the illusion that all of us are stationary while the world is moving beneath us like a treadmill.

9:23 a.m.

Are they building a prison up ahead? Concrete walls with metal rebar reflect white in the morning sun. What a strange place to build a prison, surrounded by office buildings. High barbed-wire fences surround the construction.

No, it's not a prison. The sign has a picture of an office complex that looks just like the rest of them. School, office jobs, prison. At least in prison, they don't pretend you're free.

9:30 a.m.

I'm not even out of the city, and I'm wearing out. Maybe it's the sugary energy drink in my empty stomach. Have I already crashed and burned? I'm hungry, and the advertisements everywhere lie about what the food is going to look like. I'm tired of fake food. I need something real. Is there even anything real? And also quick? And also cheap?

I can't help but notice how every few exits have the same fast-food chains. Is it like this everywhere? When I get to Montana, will I find my rock in the parking lot of a Taco Bell?

C'mon, truck.

What is the rule for following behind another vehicle? I'm sure it's not the space I'm squeezed in. The cars in the fast lane are going the speed of light. The cars to the right are either entering or exiting, and I'm stuck in the middle behind this semi going 65 in a 70. I can't see anything behind this thing.

C'mon, truck.

C'mon, cars, let me in the fast lane.

9:40 a.m.

An hour in.

I'm amazed at how constant the city is. How long it is. How it is its own concrete ecosystem. School buses are taking kids on field trips. Where?

Can it be called a field trip if there are no fields? My playlist has already started over, and after the stress of the city, I'm ready for something new.

I scan through radio channels from the edge of the city, through the thinning traffic at 75 mph. It's almost all talk. Not commercial talk or political talk, but people just sitting there blabbing into a microphone. Only the Christian and Tejano stations seem to be playing music. There's a song I haven't heard in a while. "Black hole sun, won't you come." Is it that or "black hole, son, won't you come"? No, I think it's talking about the sun. I try to picture my place in the universe, and the song seems to fit.

A semi is a good distance in front of me, coming on the entrance ramp and, for a moment, going the same speed as the train to the right. Two comets coming close to each other on their orbital paths. All the cars have homes, revolving from home world to work world and back. I'm a faint attempt at a ray of light escaping a black hole sun. Or driving straight into it. Or I am it.

Loud commercials.

Talk, talk, commercials, Christian, talk, talk, Tejano.

I turn the music down, and the hunger in my empty stomach gets louder. The adrenaline is wearing off, and the sugar crash allows only a few shooting stars of thought—mainly in noticing how the countryside is not the city. I get glimpses of understanding of what the city is by contrast with its opposite. I find a station playing an unfamiliar but catchy song and turn it up.

10:10 a.m.

Still flipping through the radio stations.

A group of small birds flits across my field of view, catching my attention. They are the first birds I've seen, and they draw my eyes toward the sky. I look at the clock and compare it to the position of the sun. I imagine the line of its path and the line that I'm driving, wondering if there's a point at which they'll cross.

A vulture circles in the far west.

Commercial. Talk, talk, commercial, preacher. I listen to the preacher for a few minutes, then flip through the ad-laden stations and rest for a few minutes on one with a salesman speaking in animated Spanish. I get a sense that they are somehow related. I've had a year of Spanish and a childhood of church, so I can pick up on a few words and phrases. Still, neither makes much sense. A scissortail races across my view, and I look up and out again. Those were Grandpa's favorite. Now there are two vultures gliding overhead in the otherwise blank sky. I feel a thought coming on, but my phone rings. It's my girlfriend.

"Where are you?"

"On the road."

"Who are you with?"

"It's just me."

"Why are you listening to Tejano music?"

I turn it down and try to think of a smart answer.

"Where are you?" she asks again.

"I think I'm in Wichita Falls."

"What?! Why are you . . . What's going on? You'd better . . ."

I stop listening and enter survival mode as a sudden rush of traffic makes me brake and check my mirrors. Trying to interrupt and tell her I'll call her back later, I lose my road awareness and accidentally take an exit.

"I gotta go," I finally blurt and hang up. There's a U-turn sign up ahead, and I get in that lane to pass under the bridge. Food. There's a burger joint under the highway and a strong empty presence in my stomach and in my head.

"Number one with large fries and a Coke," I say into the intercom, then pull up to the window.

As a smiling, older Black lady hands me my drink, she must sense that I'm going somewhere. That or she noticed that I'm in a car. "Where ya headin', hon'?"

"Montana," I reply without thought or pause.

"Ya got a ways to go. Be careful."

There's something comforting in her motherly tone. I pull into a parking space and scarf down the burger. With food in my stomach, I resolve to go on. My foot feeds gas to the engine as a renewed surge of adrenaline takes me back on the highway, veering north.

I open Spotify, turn up the music, and sing at the top of my lungs.

10:40 a.m.

The hard and fast music I love seems to outpace the car's speed as what seemed like fast at first is starting to feel slow. With a twinge of musical anxiety, I quiet the phone and flip through the radio stations again in a vain attempt to find something new. There is nothing new. Only so many notes, so many words, so many sounds.

A great white bird grabs my attention and draws it to the changing environment.

The usual trees, whatever kind they are that grow everywhere in Texas, have thinned out into farmlands and fields. Much of the grazing land is green against the cloudless blue sky, with cows huddled in close groups. Every small bridge I drive over is home to small, playful birds that seem to enjoy chasing each other and racing over, under, and around the road. I look expectantly for my yellow cockatiel among them.

The map on my phone turns me due north onto a two-lane highway through more fields with new growth, clumps of cows, and power lines. I've never really paid that much attention to scenery before. Well, I've never been around much scenery other than the city, but in noticing the power lines, I wonder if I've ever seen a landscape without them.

11:00 a.m.

I'm tired of flipping through the stations again, giving a few minutes even to the ads and the talkers—end of the world (ugh), news (fires somewhere, terrorism threat, talk of war), furniture on sale.

"How do you listen to Gaawd? He doesn't speak always to the mind or emotions, but byyyy the Spirit tooooo the spirit. And not always through the church or preachah, but through everydaaay people and even things you see or experience."

Why do preachers always pronounce it *Gawd*? Is it a Texas thing? I'm driving through a few miles of fields with nothing happening in them. Not even cows. Is that the Spirit speaking to me? I don't get it.

That trailer off in the brush with the solar panels and a hammock between two short trees—I get that. The vulture, waiting for something to die so it can scavenge its next meal. Like the news, right? I get that too.

God trying to talk to me? I don't get that.

CHAPTER 4

FRIDAY MORNING:
OKLAHOMA

11:11 a.m.

I always heard the **Red River** was really red, but I never thought about it actually being a physical river and actually being physically red. I guess some things don't really register as reality until you see them in person. People draw maps of reality. Maps . . . Reality. Somewhere there's a disconnect. It's one thing to study and know a map, but a whole other thing to experience what is mapped in real life. I scored perfect in our middle school Maps, Charts, and Graphs competition, but I've never had to actually use one to find my way around. My phone does all that for me.

And just like that, I'm in a different state. I'm not sure what I was expecting, crossing into another state, but I take inventory and—I don't feel any different. Some things around me are different. A sign warns of shrinking shoulders and narrowing lanes. The roads seem older. The speed limit changes to 65, then 55, then construction signs slow me to 45 mph for the next ten miles.

I do feel a change. I feel like the car is crawling down the road I wanted to go so fast and so far on. I'm just beginning this escape, and now, going this slow feels somehow like I'm forwardly going backward.

I study the environment without meaning to. Red soil peeks out where grass isn't growing. Power lines. Mountains in the distance. On one side of the road, an old wooden barn and farmhouse fall apart, a tractor and equipment rust their usefulness into history. On the other side, there's a new green tractor in a red metal barn and a clean white pickup parked in front of a house that would fit in in Highland Park.

Going this slow on a road intended for speed is dreadful.

11:30 a.m.

Drifting in and out of thought, I don't notice what is playing or being said or sold on the radio. The more cows, birds at bridges, fields, and trees I see, the more they become like the radio: nothing new. I do notice that every little town has a railroad crossing.

Finally. A big town is coming up. I was so ready to get out of the city environment, and now I'm excited about getting back to it. Really? Recognizable stores line both sides of the road: Walmart, Pizza Hut, McDonald's. Other businesses are the same type, just with names I don't recognize. Stoplights and traffic.

People in machines. Are they just parts in a larger machine? Going to work, coming home, going to work, coming home? Or are they more like blood pumping through a body, stopping and going in circles with the beat of the heart? But what would be the heart?

I turn down the radio to put up my driving defenses and make sure I don't get a speeding ticket in Oklahoma. I've heard the cops in Oklahoma love ticketing Texans.

Hints of silence at the stoplights take turns with the sound of the tires and engine as I speed back up—like calming exhales and anxious breaths. I'm past the town already, and now I realize I'm getting low on fries and soda. I won't turn around for food. What *would* I turn around for? What would I keep going for? I crank up the radio and keep my finger above the search button, punching it every few minutes.

What looked like mountains in the distance earlier now start to just look like big hills. A mirage on the road in front of and behind me looks like water, except it recedes at the same rate I get nearer. I think back to science class, learning about the heat rising from the road and disturbing the light waves. My past. My future. A random line from freshman English comes to mind: "Water, water everywhere, but not a drop to drink."

I have a brief standoff with a vulture eating bloodied meat in the middle of my lane. I don't slow down, and it just looks at me. I brace for a thud of impact, but it lumbers to the shoulder, then spreads its long wings and flaps hard to get off the ground. I watch in the rearview mirror as it returns to its meal. Another line from somewhere in English class comes to mind: "Because I could not stop for death—it kindly stopped for me."

Huh. I guess I paid attention more than I thought, but I can't tell what it means or how they all relate—much less who said what or where it's from. Mr. Adams would just repeat the line like it was something that could be understood if he said it enough . . . slowly, with hand motions.

The road lulls me back deep into the seat. The mountains that became hills now become giant eroded rocks, holding on to the memory of mountains. From dust they came, and to dust they return. Future people will eat the cows that eat the grass that grows in the dirt that used to be the sand that eroded from those used-to-be mountains.

11:55 a.m.

I slow to a stop where the northbound highway tees in a town named Granite. The town sprouts out of a curve in a long rock hill just tall enough to be fun to run up. I suppose it must be made of granite. The highway tees again at a stop sign in front of a meat processing plant. I turn west and pass through the town more quickly than I came to it.

12:00 p.m.

I come to another decision-making stop sign, this time with a choice of taking 283 north or south. Doing the math, I figure I can make it back and park my dad's car in his spot without him even noticing, if I turn back now. Another vulture dines in the road directly in front of me. We stare each other down. Is there meaning in this? Is this what my parents are going to do to me if I continue on this meaningless escape? Or is the vulture telling me that life is short and I should continue? It's not going to make me think about Grandpa. By the time I give up on analyzing the vile creature, I am already ten miles north.

Scanning the radio hopelessly for a variation in music and blabber, I notice the signs on the road aren't matching the directions on the phone. I'm on a well-paved road, but it's running through a stretch of land that seems like it was abandoned decades ago. There are vines and bushes growing on unrepaired fences and overgrown trees. Abandoned farmhouses and vehicles slowly yield to gravity and growth. Old fields that might have grown hay now host a messy competition of plants vying for space. The eerie lack of power lines and people makes me feel like I've entered a twilight zone. Are the mesas in the distance the same hills I passed not too long ago? This driving is messing with my head.

A human is stranded up ahead, leaning under the hood of his new pickup. Even if this isn't an alternate universe, I don't know how to help and really don't want to interact with anyone. I thoughtfully swerve into the oncoming lane to give him some space as I check my gas gauge and speed on.

I haven't gone through much gas, but it sure feels like a lot of time has passed. I think about the relativity of "gas time," which affects people in different cars going different speeds and for different purposes differently.

I am in over my own head. My mind is grasping for thoughts. Entertainment? Is that what the brain does when there isn't an overload of traffic, signs, music, and commercials? The twilight zone seems to be behind me now as the scenery comes back to a relative normal. Grass, cows, fences, power lines.

On one side of the road is some sort of grass, all the same height and type, rippling on the top like water does on the lake. On the other side is a field that has turned into what reminds me of a classmate's nappy dreadlocks. They switch sides.

On the left, there is kind of a pseudo forest of tall dead trees with new young ones growing beneath them.

Typical farmsteads, typical songs, typical variation of fields—empty, growing, cut and dried, and untended. Typical cows, typical birds, and typical power lines. Are these power lines connected somehow to the ones back home?

I need a restroom, and there's a tractor slowing me and several other cars into an impatient line. I picture everyone stopping at the next gas station and getting out for the restroom, only the tractor driver got there first, and no one knew he was going to have to pass a kidney stone while we wait, squirming.

[Sayre—5 miles]

12:20 p.m.

I was right—the tractor and half the cars turned in at the first gas station. I don't stop, but I let the pull of my engine slow me down. I look for a coffee shop in a town that, by the look of the downtown storefronts, was booming a hundred years ago. I find one east of the intersection. I park, stretch to the sky, and run across traffic to find the restroom.

I walk in and realize how uncomfortable it can be, entering a new place in a new town as a new face. The two baristas turn and study me, instantly recognizing I'm not a local. I peer back at them as a stranger, then look around the room. Some country song about drinking in the middle of the day plays softly on the radio, but it seems loud compared to the whispery conversations around the tables. Odd that, during the lunch hour, there are so many more seats than people in a town with so many more buildings than businesses.

"Large black coffee and a scone please," I say to the baristas' backs as I trot past them to the restroom.

After emptying my bladder, I'm a new person. I sip the hot coffee, get back behind the wheel, and speed out of town. My own revitalized pulse makes me think about that town's dying pulse. There was just a little life in that town, growing inside the falling bricks of generations past. I wonder what it was like in its youth and what caused the change. Did it graduate and not know what to do next? Could it have made different decisions and turned out better? Or was it out of its own control, like maybe a new highway was built somewhere else and people just traveled a different way? Is there hope for new life in Sayre? Or is it like the fields?

Fields. Some cut. Some plowed. Some green. Some returning to nature. Power lines. The highway signs have teepees on them.

I turn up the radio. "And I still . . . haven't found . . . what I'm looking for." I feel like I've heard this song before. Does that mean he is looking for something but just hasn't found it, or that he doesn't even know what he's looking for? For now, I'm content just looking without looking for.

The wind blows over the grass tips and to an old, turning metal windmill. Giant wind turbines rotate slowly in the distance. Here I am, chasing the wind, while people have found ways to harness the force and make it work for them. Civilization wins.

The sign says Cheyenne is up ahead. Wasn't that a Native tribe? Will I be driving through a reservation? Do they still use teepees? I feel dumb not knowing. All I know are the stereotypes and what

I've seen in movies. How am I supposed to know any different? Do they think all Texans ride their horses to work and wear cowboy hats?

I'm not really hungry for food, but I take little bites from the scone I got in the whispering coffee shop as if it will fill me. The scone feeds my body; my eyes feed my brain. I'm struck by how different from each other these uncultivated landscapes can be—naturally beautiful at one turn and raw, unkempt disorder at the next. Over one hill, the sky rests on lush green valleys with dirt so red I mistake the bare patches for wildflowers. Over the next, piles of dead trees and mangled bushes that warn this is no place for man.

Occasionally, I climb over a taller hill that offers a glimpse of a larger picture—miles and miles of green, rolling hills covered in farms, ranches, and unconquered prairies. I'm the only one on the road now. Just me, the radio, and the vultures. If I get in a wreck, I hope I'm thrown from the car so the hideous birds can return me to nature. I don't want to be embalmed and kept from it.

An old motorcycle is stuck up on top of a ten-foot pole. There are so many things I want to take pictures of and share, but I have no time or desire to stop.

"Lean on me . . . when you're alone . . . and you need a friend . . . we all need somebody . . . to lean on."

No. The longer I drive, the more I realize I need to be alone. I don't need a friend. I've been leaning on people all my life. Friends have been leaning on me. I don't *know* alone. I've never liked being alone. I've never wanted to be alone. But it's kinda nice.

Cheyenne is just another small town with pulses of life in old buildings standing like monuments to remind people of a time in the past. There are no teepees or signs of Native life. Native history seems to be preserved only in highway signs and names of towns. Maybe *cheyenne* is a color.

Getting tired of the noise, I turn off the radio. But the silence makes me feel like I'm going slower than I am. So I turn it back on, just not as loud.

Changing channels gives me something to do as I wait for the hills with the briefly larger view.

In elementary school, we learned about the Great Plains being the "breadbasket of America" and colored it yellow with pictures of grain. I was expecting nothing but flat fields of hay. I've enjoyed the winding roads and small changes in the scenery, looking forward to groups of birds at the bridges. There's been enough variation for me to look with interest without looking for anything in particular. But even still, the more of it there is, the more it starts to feel the same.

The red dirt is slowly changing to light brown. Wind blows through the trees, tumbles over the fields of baled hay on one side of the road, and makes waves in the young grass on the other. I'm going the same speed, but it feels slower. The station is going out.

Out of nowhere, a big testosterone truck speeds around from behind and startles me to attention. I grip the wheel tighter, but just as quickly as it appeared, it speeds away. Why do some people need to prove they're bigger than other people? Cooler, richer? I feel like I'm better than them by not trying to prove it, but isn't that the same thing?

I'm on a long, old, cement bridge that spans a floodplain, and an uneasy feeling comes over me. Why? The rhythmic bumps of the bridge gaps are jarring. I roll down the window and find another station playing a melodic electric guitar. I think it's Guns N' Roses or maybe someone else with a whiny, raspy voice. "Love is all around" he sings, but I'm alone. I'm not even sure what love is.

1:25 p.m.

Dust blows over the road from the west. The bales of hay, the huddled cows, and the vultures don't notice. The sun is beating down on my arm. There is no cell service, only five radio stations, and the only one playing music is country.

A fire burns in the east. A fast fire and slow smoke, billowing to the clouds. I've seen illustrations of Native American smoke signals, but now I can imagine it. I feel a connection to the fire. Or the smoke. I lose the thought with the realization that a semi has seated itself on my tail. Sunlight reflects off the dozens of metal parts in my mirrors. The wind pushes me on and off the grooved shoulder, making it sound like a tire's blown out. A radio commercial blares for my attention as I try to change stations (but only make the AC blow harder).

I've got the cruise set to the speed limit, but the semi pushes my heartbeat faster. Tight hands, the smoke shifts, wind pushes, AC blasts, radio blares, and the glare from the mirrors blinds me. I slow to the short shoulder to let the hungry monster pass.

[Flammable]

Goodbye, truck. Radio off. Windows down. I watch the smoke signals rise in the east. Deep breaths. Back on the road.

Speed up.

Slow down.

New town.

[Arnett, Oklahoma]

A water tower with a picture of a wildcat. Have all the water towers I've passed had town mascots on them? Are there wildcats here? A street is named Van Buren. The president? What was his policy on Natives?

Questions I wonder but don't give much effort to ponder (except to notice there is a difference).

Grasslands.

More state highway signs with teepees.

Grasslands.

Just when I give up on my expectation of the elementary mapped breadbasket of America image, I come upon the flat plains of eternal boredom.

Grasslands.

Finally, a hill. Three crosses on top of it. I wonder, but don't ponder.

Silent radio.

Thought.

I don't know what to think. The scenery has stopped entertaining.

There is nothing to distract me.

I think about calling my girlfriend or friends, but they're still in school. Has it really not been that long? I have no service, anyway.

What do people think about when they have the opportunity to think?

Wind over the flat land and in the sparse trees.

Is there any spot on this land that hasn't been walked on before by humans?

Is it possible to think a thought no one has ever thought before?

Are thoughts just responses to the environment?

Every thought I start to think is like an all-too-familiar radio station commercial I can't wait to change, even if it means coming back to it only to pass it by. Same thoughts. They are all meaningless.

Bright sun.

Nothing new.

Is this why I hate silence?

I'm not going to turn on the radio.

Not going to think about Grandpa.

Not going to think about Mom and Dad.

Not going to think about being yelled at and grounded for the rest of the year. They wouldn't kick me out. They know I'd enjoy it.

My breadbasket tightens. I'm hungry. I hate that book.

Good, a town is coming up.

[Shattuck Indians]

A town with a mascot that fits its geography. I wonder if there are any Indians here.

2:00 p.m.

The first impression of Shattuck is the water tower that says it again: Indians. Isn't it politically incorrect to call them Indians? Mrs. Lopez taught us in elementary to call them Natives, that they didn't like being called Indians. She said it is like calling her Latina instead of Mexican, even though she was from Mexico. My friend Arcadio likes to be called Mexican even though he's second-generation American. It's like how some African Americans get mad if you call them Black, and others get mad if you don't. Or is it that only the Indians can call each other Indians, but others are supposed to call them Natives?

The whole political correctness thing wears me out. There's no way to play it safe. Either be yourself and accidentally offend someone, or try not to offend someone and come across as restrained and awkward. Or maybe it's a town that's all White that didn't get the memo and just hasn't been sued yet.

A truck stop designed as a giant teepee welcomes travelers with giant lettering above the convenience store entrance: "El Tipi." Is that Spanish? The empty parking lot and perched vultures are not welcoming.

[Business District]

I drive past blocks and blocks of cemetery. Is this the business district? The lichened tombstones turn into lichened buildings. A windmill museum displays monuments of machinery past and present. A liquor store. A night club. I feel bad for admitting that this might be a town with actual Native presence, then sad as I pass a leather-skinned old man drinking from a brown paper bag as slow as he is walking.

Am I racist because the stereotypes stood out to me? But I didn't make the gas station a teepee, and I didn't make any Natives drink. Or would it only be racist if I see a Native and automatically assume he lives in a teepee and is an alcoholic? I really don't want to be racist, and I don't think I am, but it's just such a confusing subject. It's so easy to say the wrong thing and so explosive when you do. I don't even feel safe thinking about these things.

Railroads cross the road, *thump thump*, under me, and I'm out of the town.

Tempted to turn on the radio, I already know it has nothing to offer. I give an honest effort at thinking. Small towns and history . . . People, heritage, and history. How the past affects the present.

There's so much I don't know. But what good would knowing do?

Another cross on a hill, this time just one. Is it God speaking to me, or was it planted like a flag, claiming territory for manifest destiny in Indian land?

Sandy hills make the plains more entertaining for a few miles.

A splash of purple wildflowers gives me hope of change.

No more purple flowers. I should have loved them more.

My coffee is pretty cold now.

Two trees with a road between. Why is one dead and the other fully alive? Aren't they in the same soil? Don't they get the same amount of sun and water?

The grass is really greener to the east.

Cows huddle.

The tires get quiet on the pavement.

Old farm equipment rusts.

A white-and-gray hawk flies from a fencepost.

No thoughts. No one on the road. No change in scenery. There are only trees where there is water.

A car comes into sight slowly, then zooms by. Where are they going? Am I the only one who doesn't know?

As my mind gives up, waves of sadness overwhelm me.

Anger.

Happy bridge birds swarm. Twenty or more vultures circle above the trees.

Rough road. Big bumps.
Cold coffee. Scone is gone.
No service.
It's only 2:20?

2:20 p.m.

Radio on.

Intentional grooves and bumps in the pavement warn road-dazed drivers of a stop ahead. I sit at the stop sign at the intersection of 283 and 270/412 and catch my breath. Distant cars, one coming from each direction. The point at which we meet is the point we all change direction. *Ooh, a good thought!* But what does it mean?

It's like I know there's deep soil and even bedrock far below, but all I can see is the grass.

A bare tree in front of me stands as its own memory of its last reach to the sky for hope of life.

[Laverne Tigers]

I'm pretty sure there are no tigers here. Natives either. Radio off. An old man with a thick, white Fu Manchu peels out of the gas station lot in his souped-up classic muscle car. I imagine it is sixty years ago and the car is as new as it looks. The old man is young, heading for Montana. The good old days.

Today is tomorrow's good old days.

There's no way when I'm eighty, I'll fully restore a Hyundai to show off.

A pioneer museum and some log-cabin style buildings catch my eye as I realize that not every town has had a Walmart, Taco Bell, McDonald's, or CVS. Most of the main businesses in these smaller towns seem to be directly related to agriculture. Never heard of any of them. I drive over railroad tracks and am past the town.

Working windmills pull water to a trough. Cows huddle as birds rest on their backs.

Beaver River is dry.

No new thoughts as my mind searches for signs and changes in scenery. A new type of tree. Some kind of cedar? Must be due to rainfall or temperature?

How is that a thought? It's just a response with the logic I know. How is that different from reading books and reacting? How is how I feel about a book important? I feel like all Mr. Adams wants is for us to read and feel something or think something.

I'm just feeling angry. Angry and tailing a truck. It's just me and him on the road, and I'm in a hurry. It must look funny from above, miles of empty road and two cars nearly touching, going the same direction. All that road and not enough room. All this road and not enough seconds.

I slow down. The teepee highway signs have been replaced with a scissortail or some kind of bird. Am I in a new state? I search the sky and the power lines for that kind of bird but don't see any. Is it to commemorate a native bird that's now been hunted to extinction?

The truck slows to a stop sign that I can't see.

[283] [Dodge City]

Excited at a city with a familiar name, I wonder if it is anything like the movies. The truck turns right; I turn left toward Dodge.

Waves of green. Splotchy brush. Cut fields. Dry grass. Just me and the road.

Just me and the road.

Me. And the road.

Is the car on autopilot, or am I?

Happiness. What is happiness? I don't know. Not unhappiness.

Why am I going to Montana? I don't know. Not unMontana.

There are brief *wows* in the mundane. Is it because they are really beautiful things, or are they just beautiful because there is finally a break from the miles of same?

A red, eroded gully with an oddly placed windmill down by the water breaks the breadbasket boredom.

The map on my phone won't let me zoom out. It keeps zooming back in. I don't know where I am.

Quick vibrations on the tires tell me I'm veering off the road. Okay. Deep breath. Hands on the wheel. Eyes on the road.

The land has turned hilly. Not like big hills, but like dense bulges. Like the brushy land was kneaded and squeezed together by the fingers of giants. Then, flat.

Flat.

The next thing I know, I'm in a small town with houses but no signs, and no signs of life except an old man mowing his lawn. In fact, all the lawns in this town are mowed. Is it really his lawn he is mowing, or is he mowing the whole town? Is he the only person that lives here, keeping it looking nice, waiting for people to come back? Did he build his own utopia, hoping others would join him, not giving up on his dream?

My thoughts are driving me crazy. The rails cross the road, and the old man and his empty utopia are behind me. Then, flat.

Flat, flat.

Even in silence, there is no silence.

Finally, a relief in the stretches of farmland. Rolling plains, bridges with streams and bridge birds. Bridge birds are happy. Or are they? Are they like high school? Instead of playing tag, are the boys squawking at the girls and the girls just trying to out chirp the others?

Telephone poles in the shape of crosses. I'm sure there's a metaphor there.

Is understanding a skill you have to learn or something you just get? All my life, teachers have always told us what things mean, but how do they know? From their own thoughts or because someone else told them? Or do they just make stuff up?

I think I'm in Kansas.

No farms, no cows. Did I expect everything to be functional and busy? If the dry grass were sand, it would look like the Sahara. I roll down the window to take a picture. I swear I smell cows, but as far as I can see, there isn't even one.

CHAPTER 5

FRIDAY AFTERNOON: KANSAS

3:15 p.m.

A long silence. The longest I think I've ever endured.

Uneven grassland.

My back and butt are starting to hurt. About right. By this time every day in school, I start to squirm in my seat. It means school is about out.

3:35 p.m.

I call my best friend, and it makes me feel how far from that world I really am.

"You're going to be in so much trouble!"

In the background I hear others.

"Come home!"

"You're dumb!"

"You're awesome!"

"Bring me a souvenir!"

From where I am, that world doesn't make sense. It doesn't harmonize with the tires going 65 on a slow tour of endless fields and the sky. My friends are just like the noise of the radio.

Right after I hang up, my girlfriend calls, but the signal is breaking up. I'm kind of glad, but I don't know why.

Seven hours is the longest I've ever been alone. It's the longest I can remember being quiet on purpose.

Fear of being alone makes us latch on to each other for all the wrong reasons. Fear of silence makes us fill our heads with distraction.

I slow to a stop at Junction 54 toward Minneola. My gut pulls tight again. Acid seems to be collecting behind my right shoulder blade, and my left arm is burning from the sun. I sip air out of the coffee cup and feel around in the container for anything more than a crumb of the scone. Maybe

I just need food.

A red light on a radio tower blinks above a flattened, harvested field. I turn on the radio to see if it's a sign.

"Color with your family. I guarantee you'll have fun . . ."

"Israel has been provoked by Palestine . . . "

Wind on grains. The same wind blows on the Palestinians as they hurl rockets at Israel. Do they notice it?

They should color instead.

Celtic music . . . Green hills of Ireland. Do they look like these hills? Could I have entered a wormhole? Am I actually driving through Ireland? Or anywhere?

Spanish rock and roll. What does Spain look like?

A crazy-sounding lady makes bold judgments. Why do so many Christians talk so crazy?

Spanish rap . . . Country girl . . . Hip hop . . .

"Those who really love you will never leave you . . . "

Yes, they will.

I'm at a stop sign in Dodge City at an intersection, and I don't know which road to follow. I'm angry. Why? I don't know. Time to park and stretch my legs. Food.

The highway leads right into parking lots for what seems to be downtown. There's no skyline or skyscrapers. Just rows of old brick and stone buildings, probably built before elevators existed. The entire strip faces the parking lots.

Maybe I'm in the Old West. Train tracks. Wooden storefronts, steel cutouts of revolvers, big glass windows with posters and pictures of Wyatt Earp and Doc Holliday. Lawmen, bandits, horse thieves, bank robbers.

Looking for a saloon-style restaurant to get a steak in while the piano plays itself.

The more I walk, the more I realize the facade is just that. The local flavor of the Old West turns out to be a Chinese buffet, Italian, and Mexican food. The city, in name and appearance, is a monument to a time that no longer exists.

I retrace my steps, planning to explore the other direction, but anxiety overwhelms me. The people and sounds are making my head swim. Two gangster-looking guys blow cigarette smoke as they lean against a pole with a steel cutout of a cowboy leaning against it.

Clang, clang, clang! The sounding horn of the train. The cars whizzing by. The conflict of my expectations and reality. I retreat to the car, where it is quiet. I pull out of the parking lot and follow the tracks west.

[Montana Steaks]

The sign announces the steak I am craving, but I'm not there yet. Instead, I pull into a small coffee shop across the street, still hungry and a little confused about my expectations of the city so tied to the memory of the rugged Old West.

After looking over the menu, I ask the shy barista for a chicken sandwich and a large coffee. "Make yourself at home," she says as she turns toward the kitchen.

I don't want to be home. That's why I'm here.

I tour the converted house, looking for the restroom. The worn, old hardwood floors creak as I walk around. Are these creaks the only thing that still speaks from the past?

I make a home at a table in a room filled with "Western art by Western artists." A folded placard stands on the table. St. Francis Community Service. "The answer is a parent."

The quiet barista appears with my sandwich and a kind smile. I try to eat it with delicate appreciation. Is it really that good, or am I just that hungry? At camp a few summers ago, there was this scrawny kid who let all the bigger, more aggressive teenagers cut in front of him at mealtime.

"Are you sure?" I asked him one time, feeling a little bad but not bad enough to let him go first.

"Hunger is the best spice," he replied with a forced smile.

I was hungry and cut ahead of him with my friends. I wonder what he's like now. Did he have a growth spurt and now pushes people out of the way to get to the front? My sandwich is gone. So much for delicate appreciation.

Back in the car, I try radio silence. With a deep breath and full stomach, a little caffeine and sugar, I'm ready for the calming sound of the road through the peaceful plains. And the phone rings. It's my girlfriend.

"Hello?"

"Where are you? Are you on your way back?"

"I just left Dodge City, and no, not yet."

"Are you okay? I'm worried about you. What's going on?"

"I can't explain, but I'll be back Sunday."

"Red! What on earth? Where are you going? This is so unlike you—"

"I don't know. You're cutting out."

I hang up the phone. A tightness pulls in my chest. What *is* going on? Where *am* I going? This *is* so unlike me. Am I okay? I could turn around and make it back tonight. A bird flies in front of my windshield, and I brace for a broken window. At the last moment, it swoops upward, and I look back to watch it land gently on a fence. Another bird does the same thing. These birds are surfing the air from my car!

I look out for more surfing birds and take in the horse ranches. I picture the old Westerns taking place here in color. A silhouette cutout of a team of horseback riders is on top of a hill overlooking a rugged plain.

I stop in Cimarron at the grocery store for some snacks and earplugs. They don't have earplugs. As I head into town, I'm looking for the sign guiding north. The map on my phone isn't doing what it is supposed to. There's a split, and I'm sure either will work. Apparently, 50 West is the mountain route; 23 North is the Cimarron route. Mountains sound appealing, but 23 is what I was looking for . . .

Who was Cimarron?

I pass another man broken down. I just don't know what to do to help people. Windmill farms. A dairy. Manicured fields. Not much wild in the old wild West.

Birds hop on and off the road in front of me. I chuckle. Birds playing chicken. Birds on the electric wire. Ungrounded.

I'm going to be grounded when my dad finds

out I took his car. I've got less than an hour before he'll notice.

Mr. Adams said every word a great author writes is intentional, every detail meaningful. I just don't see it. How can everything have meaning? If a great writer were writing about a drive up the Great Plains, how would they find meaning in the repetition of such vast sameness? Even the slight variation becomes mundane after a while.

A new idea repeated once has lost its magic . . . if there even is such a thing as a new idea.

The longer I drive, the more of a bird's-eye view I seem to have of the land. And the more of a bird's-eyeview, the more it all seems meaningless.

5:00 p.m.

My girlfriend gets out of dance every day about this time, and we meet behind the gym to make out before I catch a ride home with my dad.

I feel bad for missing her in that way. But is she just a means to an end? Call her when I'm feeling alone; make out when I need to feel good? Is that what I am to her?

Grandpa told me when I first started taking an interest in girls that the purpose of a relationship was for two people to make each other better humans. I'm not a bad guy, but I'm not perfect. I'm not sure, though, what it means to be a *better person*. I sure could use some mountains right now.

This is the flattest and plainest this drive has been. Again.

In a daze, I almost miss my turn.

* * *

Mirages.

I'm the only one on the road.

My shoulder blades are on fire.

The afternoon sun beats through my window.

I should call Dad. He'd be easier to talk to. How is he going to get home?

I should wait for him to call.

[Pawnee River]

Flat green scenery.

Straight road to the horizon. Nothing new. I'll call at six.

Knowing there may have been a mountain route makes this one seem even more dreadfully boring. But if I were there, wouldn't I get tired of that as well?

I feel like I am slowly slowing while the grass is slowly growing.

I've already thought about birds, fields, power lines . . .

Thoughts are becoming like the radio, flipping through looking for something new or worth listening to. But they're all the same. Nothing new. Can thoughts distract from silence as well? How long can I not think?

Wind on the grass. I've seen it for hours. I appreciate it. A prolonged silence takes over me. Not a daze, not automatic, not a dream . . . almost a consciousness. Not a conscious consciousness, not a subconscious or an unconsciousness.

In the silence, I experience it. What it is, I don't know, but it comes over me.

Something about the wind. Something about it brushing the top of me. The immensity of what wind is and how it blows over even plowed fields. How it's over and through everything. How you can't see it, but you can see the effects. How it's an outside force that causes movement. A movement that causes movement. An energy. Newton's laws.

By noticing it, I'm drawn out of it. Back to the ground, the wheels on it, and an upcoming town.

[Dighton]

Another small town with a railroad crossing.

5:30 p.m.

Zoned out. Dazed into daydream with visions of buffalo on a timeless landscape where wind stacks the sand and blows it over as grass grows and dies. Cut away.

Long horizon in all directions; the only measurement behind me.

My mind is playing tricks. I hear birds crisply chirping, interrupting bouts of dazed silence.

A fast semi approaches.

The white noise is green.

Another broken-down car. It looks a lot like

mine. Next stop, I'll buy a case of water so I have something to offer. And earplugs. I'm becoming more aware of the sleepy daze and how it over-comes me. I crave absolute silence in a way that makes me anxious.

6:00 p.m.

No service. Switching arms holding the wheel relieves one shoulder blade at a time from the ach-ing. The sun peeks from clouds I didn't notice be-fore. It is a scene of beauty, but to me right now, it's still the same sky I've been looking at for ten hours. What was I expecting?

[Gove]

[Yarn and Antiques]

[Feed and Seed]

[Jo's Photography]

Every building is in use, all three of them. This town never grew and never shrank. Towns are like people somehow. My bladder is full, and the tank is near empty.

Lesson from the snake: don't bask on the road.

There is more roadkill on this stretch, but no vultures. Where are the vultures? Are vultures regional?

Scanning for life, I see huddled cows. No, horses. Horses stick together too? What would happen if you put a pack of horses and a herd of cows in the same small space as chickens, pigs, and birds? I picture it like school. The cows and horses would battle it out like those *cholos* this morning, while the chickens scurry to stay out of the way and the pigs do nothing.

Finally, a gas station. The gas is on, but the station is closed. While the glug of the gas into the tank measures time in a new way, I realize I haven't called my parents. I leave the nozzle, sit in the car, and find my phone. It lights up with a new connection that blasts all the texts I missed.

"Where are you?"

"Your girlfriend had to give your dad a ride."

"Granddad's funeral is Sunday at 4:00. You'd better be back."

"Call us."

"Hello?"

"You're in so much trouble."

I leave the back roads and head out onto the highway. It feels good to go 75 again. No radio. A sign has a big, yellow smiley face and says, "Smile, your mom chose life." I bet she wouldn't agree right now. I smile anyway.

The sign for Oakley has the silhouette of a Native with a bow and arrow aiming to shoot a buffalo. Sunflowers have replaced the teepees and birds on the highway signs. It must not be the season for sunflowers. That or we killed them all and are honoring their memory with a picture on an official sign.

The whole trip, I haven't really sped. I got a ticket in Arlington one time going a few miles per hour over. My parents made me pay the ticket, and I swore I'd never speed again. But my mind has turned to math for entertainment. Seventy-six covers one more mile an hour. In ten hours, that saves ten minutes. Seventy-eight saves thirty. Eighty-one can save sixty. Considering I'll be driving maybe twenty hours there and back, with some sleep in between, those forty hours of going six over will get me home with even more time to spare. If my math is right, I'll shave off three, maybe four hours.

My phone buzzes six times with a new load of texts I don't want to read. I don't read texts while I'm driving—partially because of the presentations we have to sit through every year at school with crying moms and totaled cars, but mostly because I almost drove off the road one time. Anyway, I just look down to see who it was that was texting. As I look back up, lights are flashing behind me. Great.

I pull over and wait.

And wait. First police car I've seen the whole trip. Finally, the officer walks up to my window, and I roll it down.

"Where you headed so fast?"

"Montana, sir."

"For?"

"Happiness." I don't know why I said that or even if I believe it.

"License and registration."

I hand him my ID and what I think is registration. It works.

"Do you know why I am pulling you over?"

"Yessir. I was just trying to shave off some time on the long drive."

"You were going eighty-one in a seventy-five, but I pulled you over because you swerved into on-coming traffic."

My gut drops.

"Were you texting?"

"No sir," I say. Half true. My phone is still in my lap. "I think I just need to pull over and stretch my legs and get some food."

"Take that exit just ahead. You'll find plenty of places to gather yourself." He hands me the ticket and warns me not to speed. "If you want to die," he says, "that's your business. But don't kill someone else in the process."

I take the exit and pull into a 24/7 gas station, heart racing. I find relief in the restroom, then look around for some caffeine and find earplugs. I walk up to the counter, oddly excited about the earplugs. A man with frazzled white hair and a matching stringy, wild goatee catches me catching him frantically looking for something of immediate importance.

Giving up his search for whatever it was, he says, "Forget it. Everyone's in such a gosh darn hurry. I gotta go my speed. If I go my speed, everything turns out right. Rush me, and everything falls apart." Realizing I'm still watching and listening to him, he says, "Hang on." Then he takes a deep breath, closes his eyes, and collects himself.

"I've been doing this for sixteen years. I still get caught up in other people thinking little stuff is the end of the world. It's a freakin' gas station. It's meaningless, all of it."

I pay for my soda and earplugs and try to encourage the guy. "Hang in there, man. I hear you."

As I cross the tracks out of town, I squeeze the orange foam earplugs into thin spears and put them in my ears. They slowly expand and soften the way I hear what I've heard all day. I shuffle around my bag for a missed fry, regretting not getting anything to munch on. I look up and realize the guy in the pickup truck in front of me has slowed down to turn. I slam on my brakes. He turns, sticks his head out of his window, and yells at me.

"Pay attention!"

Yes. I want to do that.

With the earplugs in, much of the road hum is blocked out. The AC is silent. I can feel the road and hear passing cars, but what stands out is the sound of the wind against the car. I couldn't hear it before, but now it is the most noticeable sound. I crave the visceral. I don't want distraction.

What if God is trying to tell me something through everything? What if everything is full of meaning? The sun is in my eyes to the west. I pull the visor to the side window and try to pay attention.

Just me and the car. No, the car is an extension of me. Just me. No, just me and the road and the scene. They are not extensions of me. Am I an extension of them? Are we both extensions of God?

I'm not sure which takes more faith to believe in.

Mind chatter. Pay attention.

The shoulders are narrow, and the ditches are deep. The sameness. What about the sameness?

Different stages of growth in a field all in the same mile. It has to have meaning. A line of cars is going slow because of me. The pressure of others wanting to pass makes me sacrifice my intent to focus, listen, and experience something deep. It's like I'm waiting for the effects of a drug to kick in. Even placebos work sometimes if the participant believes, right?

I know something's not right with me. I'm not right inside. I don't want to exist. No, I do want to exist, just not like this.

As dull as the drive has become, it is more than the emptiness I feel. Take away my school, parents, friends, and teachers, and what am I? Take away the radio, the sounds, the thoughts, and what am I left with? Take away the cows, grass, towns, and power lines, and deep down the earth is just rock.

Hills, flats, cows, birds. There is deep bedrock lying under them. Underlying. This will be torture if God has set it up so the Great Plains don't end until I figure it out.

It bothers me that there is all this roadkill and no vultures. I look for them as if they hold the answer.

Yuccas. Those are new. If that's even what they are. Steeper hills, greener grass. Different trees. Did I figure something out? Has God moved me to the next stage?

[Atwood, Kansas—Where People Care]

[Meth Watch]

On the telephone poles, metal warning signs trying to deter crime.

[No Trespassing]

A pier juts out into an empty lake. Grass is growing on the bottom like it hasn't been a lake for a while. It isn't what it's supposed to be. It surrounds a golf course.

Meth addicts and an exclusive golf course in a town where people care enough to describe it as a town "where people care." A lake without water. I ponder how it's all related.

Leaving Atwood, I enter a picturesque scenery

with a deep vibrant green in all directions. What would all this look like if it were left alone for a thousand years? What would I become if left alone for a thousand years?

I'm beginning to like some of the thoughts I find my mind thinking, but I'm also frustrated because they seem to short circuit just after I think them. I feel like I'm asking deep questions, but the dock extends to a pond that's been dry since it was dug.

Teachers always tell us to think, but it seems more like they're preparing us for a golf tournament in which they're rated on how well we play.

I roll the window down. The air is cool and brisk.

CHAPTER 6

FRIDAY NIGHT: NEBRASKA

7:49 p.m.

The speed limit slows to 60. That's fine; I feel good. Another dimension of beauty. Awe again. What changed? The lighting? The rock deep beneath the soil? Or is it just that the scenery changed? Would I feel the same if the past four hours were like this and the landscape was finally emptying out into a straight flatness?

It doesn't take long for the answer to become clear as the amazement wears off, as if it were just an endorphin rushing through the body and dissipating and filtering into my bladder. Even still, around every few curves and over every few hills, the connection with nature reignites, even if it is a brief flame.

Quietness takes over, as if it were a sound unto itself. The cool air through the vent needs no fan. The Nebraska roads are smooth and soft. The wind must be at my back. But there is a distinct high-pitched humming. It almost sounds like my ears are ringing, but not quite. It's not coming from the car or outside.

A science teacher told us once that there is no such thing as silence where there is matter. Even the rocks emit a high-pitched sound. He said if we ever stood in a perfectly quiet place, we would hear the hum of our own body existing. The idea that I might be hearing myself exist is mind boggling. It's unfortunate—or perhaps appropriate—that it's high pitched and obnoxious.

I can't deal. The earplugs are out.

Wow. The wind on the car is loud and obvious. Funny how it stood out when I first put the earplugs in. Just because I don't hear it doesn't mean it's not there.

The hills ascend and descend like a roller coaster, and the contrast from low to high visibility is magnificent. The trees are getting taller and thicker, and I try to remember what, if anything, I know about Nebraska. Did the Oregon Trail pass through here? Grandpa had a game on his giant old computer called *The Oregon Trail* that I used to play. I just remember it had really bad graphics and you could hunt buffalo. I always lost because everyone in my covered wagon died of dysentery or something crazy.

I take a detour to drive over a long dam near Trenton. Talk about narrow shoulders and deep drop-offs! I slow way down and try to remember to look at the road instead of the sun's artistry across the rippling water. It's the biggest lake I've ever seen. At the base of the dam below are houses and fields that would be a hundred feet underwater if the dam gave way. I pull off the dam and into a parking lot with picnic tables and public access to the lake. I need to nibble on what all of it would mean if it meant something. Two men are fishing in a small metal boat. I can't help but think they get it. I can't even imagine. My pier doesn't reach the water. I pull out of the lot and back to the road marked with a state sign decorated with the silhouette of a covered wagon.

At a stop sign, a man driving an RV west waves to me as he pulls forward on his adventure. I wave back and silently hope he makes it to Oregon without losing anyone to typhoid. There are quite a few mobile homes, trucks pulling livable trailers, and trucks with beds converted into shelter. I feel like an escapee from *Sim City* who's temporarily jumped not only games but platforms. What game am I playing, and how do I win? Or, more real to my feeling, how do I not lose?

Deer on the road. Deer to the sides. I am paying attention. I smile for no reason.

Teepee structures stand as art. Just like most people I know, I'm one one-somethingth Native American. *Indian.* "History is written by the victor," my history teacher told us. We didn't learn much about Natives. In elementary, we dressed up like Indians for plays and played cowboys and Indians at recess. But then we were taught we were supposed to say Natives. I asked, "Why?" and was told to quit asking so many questions.

We're taught to ask questions, just not the tough ones and not too many. Just like we're told to think, but not given a chance to learn how to. Maybe Grandpa was right: video games really do make you stupid. Or maybe he was wrong—they didn't make me stupid; they just kept my mind occupied so I never got bored enough to feel the need to go fishing.

A roadrunner dashes across the road, waking me out of thought. No, it wasn't a roadrunner, but it moved like one. It looked more like a turkey. A dodo? What else is out there that I've never seen or imagined?

One day in history class, our teacher went on a long tangent talking about how the Spanish explorers had to rewrite all of their books because they found a pink dolphin in the Amazon River. Until then, their scientific books clearly stated that dolphins were saltwater creatures and were always shades of gray. The existence of pink freshwater dolphins made them throw out everything they knew about classification and how nature worked.

I had no idea what he was talking about, but the whole class always felt a strong victory the longer we kept him off topic. He'd always finish with "Well, we've wasted a chunk of curriculum time, but with the hope that you've learned something, it's never a waste."

An old cowboy has parked his pickup and is leaning against the fence facing a fantastic view to the west. It's still at least an hour before sunset. What is he going to do for an hour? What will he think? Does he do this every day? Did his teacher once tell him he couldn't find happiness on a fence in Nebraska?

A vulture glides up and down from behind a hill as the sun tucks behind the clouds.

The sky becomes more visible than the land beneath it.

Silence.

The silence is messing with me. I swear I hear birds chirping again. Loud and clear, as if they're in the car with me.

A hawk swoops across the road, looks me in the eyes, and shouts "CAW." Maybe my mind isn't messing with me. But how can the sound of a bird cut through the wind and roaring of the road and penetrate the substance of my car?

Mom calls. I listen, expecting the tongue lashing, trying not to shut down and shut her out. I want to explain, but what can I say? It just comes out, "Mom, I know you won't understand, but please. Just trust me that I need this."

Do I tell her about feeling the wind on the top of my soul? Do I ask her if she's ever heard a bird chirp through the windshield or the sound of her own existence? I already know how ridiculous it would sound if I told her I left because I got mad at my English teacher. Why did I leave? Am I really trying to find happiness? I don't even know that happiness will be enough. I feel empty. I feel crowded.

"Trust you? With all you've pulled this year, I'm supposed to trust you? I can't believe you! You just stole your dad's car, and who knows where you are, and—"

"I'm in Nebraska, if that's helpful."

"Helpful?! It would have been helpful if you'd have—"

"Can I talk to Dad?"

She yells across the house. Dad comes on the line.

"You're driving her crazy, Red. Don't make your mom explain to everyone that her son isn't here because he ran away. Just be back in time for the funeral."

I didn't run away. Did I? Not in the way I guess it seems. I've already missed saying goodbye to Grandpa. I don't want to miss his funeral.

"Okay, Dad. Thanks. And . . . sorry."

My first instinct is to turn on the radio. Loud. My brain is tense with anger, and my gut is tight and hurting. It's not the fast food and sugar. Okay, maybe it is. And I'm hungry. And my back hurts, right behind the shoulder blades.

As I drive toward the sunset, it keeps setting. It's the longest sunset I've ever watched. It's the only sunset I've ever watched. It hits me that driving toward it actually prolongs it.

I pass a nursery called Sunrise Heights at sunset. Is that coincidence or irony?

Just as I'm clearing my head and finding my peace, my girlfriend calls. I ask her if the sun is setting there.

"No." I can feel the tenseness in her voice.

"We're in different places; I just thought it would be cool if we were watching the same sunset." I guess we're just in different places.

We hold our phones in silence for a few minutes. My brain is empty of words to say and my heart empty of the will to say them. Finally, she splashes in. "Say something."

"I've got nothing to say."

We sit in silence a few more hour-seconds.

This time a larger splash with more waves. "What's wrong with you?!"

"I don't know." But it feels like it's bigger than me. If I can just fly a little higher and see a little farther, maybe I can spot what's dead and digest it.

Trying to listen to her stream of emotive consciousness, not hit deer, and keep my calm, I miss my turn. And I miss the rest of the sunset. I turn around on a dirt road and head back to what I missed. On this journey into peace, quiet, and solitude, I can't take the world I knew with me. I politely interrupt, "I love you," and throw the phone out the window.

Pheasants. I think they're pheasants, with the long feather in the back.

It's getting darker. The dimming leftover sunlight is making the road harder to see. Pay closer attention.

I can't tell if there are storms to the north or if those are just normal clouds at dusk.

9:00 p.m.

Chirp.

Pay attention. I need a restroom. Is it even possible to pay attention all the time? I'm trying to, but thoughts, survival, scenery, zoning out—it's hard. That would be a lower-level mutant ability on *X-Men*. I bet Jesus could do it.

Rabbit.

Houses are the only lights. Light houses. The cows are like pepper on a dark—*smack!*

That was a big bird. Dang. It was one of those roadrunner turkeys. *Pay attention!*

It gets darker still. I need to quit looking at the horizon and hills and pay attention to what is right in front of me. There has to be a metaphor in that. I'm getting good at recognizing where there might be meaning, but not at understanding it.

Unless I'm not.

Breathe.

Silence.

Nearly run off the road by an oncoming honking trucker. I forgot my brights are on.

Pay close attention. Stay awake.

Missed a turn again. There's a town. But no hotel, gas, or food. I think I expected every town to have everything. Earlier today, I was critical that every town did. Now I'm just wishing I could find a Motel 6 or a Taco Bell.

There's a well-lit place ahead. My hope grows for fast food or a cheap hotel.

[Golden Ours Convalescent Home]

What does that even mean? Golden *Ours*? Convalescent? Whatever. I just know it's not going to be my home tonight. Home. I don't need home right now. Just some food and a bed.

Note to self: clean the windshield before it gets dark.

City highways at night are never dark. Even in the short stretches between towns in Texas, I don't remember it ever being as dark as it is here. It is black outside. The only thing I can see is what's lit by my lights. When an oncoming car climbs over the horizon, the bug guts light up on my windshield, making it even harder to see.

Darkness is a metaphor. The dark times in life. The times when you can't see well. When you're surrounded by nontruth. When the soul has shut out light.

Not getting it.

Is that lightning?

Time passes in silence. I grip the wheel with both hands and lean forward, squinting, trying to see deeper into the black hole my headlights are pointed at. No headlights escape back toward me. The sign says Ogallala is coming up ahead. Isn't that an aquifer? We just studied that. This must be where the clouds enter the earth through this black hole and fill the aquifer. That must be what's going on with the sky.

Just over a hill, what looks like an underwater city reveals itself with its yellow, white, and orange streetlights, blinking red tower lights, and an oil refinery or something that looks like the town's castle. The roads are wet. I hope there is a place to stop and eat. Even the town's water tower is covered in strung lights that blink and blend with the city of lights in the dark night.

9:24 p.m.

Really, it's 10:24 without the time change. I need to remember the time changes.

I stop at an Arby's and order whatever's easiest with a large curly fry and a soda. The guy behind the counter gives me a 10 percent discount for being cool with easy.

"If you leave now," I tell him, "you'll be in Dallas by noon tomorrow."

"Is that all it is?"

Is that all it is? I wanted to tell him how long fourteen hours feels, but why argue? Why talk?

"Yeah. It's tiring." As if it mattered.

I get my food and drive carefully up the road looking for signs to follow. My phone is gone. I really could use the maps on my phone right now. Or a car with GPS. Or a brain that doesn't rely on a computer thinking for it. I think I am driving through the historic heart of the town, but it only registers as buildings and streets in my brain, no details.

I try to make the picture clearer as I write, but my imagination keeps changing what the buildings looked like. Tall and modern? Old and empty? Interspersed with houses, or am I mixing that up with another town I drove through? I don't know.

I never knew sleepiness could hurt. Severely focused on finding the right highway sign. Finally. I slowly accelerate toward two shades of black.

Lightning synapses dance ominously ahead of me.

I turn on the radio to check the weather. Nothing registers on AM. The first station on the FM is a preacher: "Be still. Listen to God." There are a few other music stations, but no weather reports. I make it back to the preacher. ". . . a humble spirit. Know what you need . . ." Back through the music stations, noise. Back to the preacher. "There are five things you need to be able to listen to God."

Is this a repeat of the same program I flipped through earlier, or is God really using the distracting noise of the radio to get through to me?

"You need to be teachable, humble, submissive, have an anticipating spirit—He really is trying to tell you something—and lastly—" The radio goes to white noise. I leave it on, hoping to catch that last thing. I'm listening. I know I need something.

Teach me!

The crackle of the radio responds to the lightning in the air—electromagnetic evidence of the power and effect of what the eyes see and can't see. Synapses fire rapidly and randomly. The sky is having thoughts. Am I driving through my own mind? And then they stop.

Not being able to see anything, I feel like I'm speeding through space. No fields of hay or grass stretching to the edge of the sky to give context. My sight is limited to the edge of the headlights, and I am anticipating a deer or roadrunner turkey. My light chest contradicts my tight fists on the wheel.

A large owl swoops by. "The owl of Minerva only flies at nightfall." Another one of Mr. Adams' deep reflections on a book I didn't read.

Miles of dark, but lights up ahead.

Hoping for a place to stop and rest . . . No, just a well-lit cemetery in the middle of nowhere. Weird.

9:45 p.m.

The storm feels so close, but I don't seem to be getting closer, which makes it seem even farther away. The lightning now shows me silhouettes of mountains. Am I close to Montana? A mole runs out on the road and looks at me.

A mole? Aren't they blind?

I am questioning my own eyes and my own mind in the darkness.

10:30 p.m.

[Bridgeport]

There is fresh rain on the ground still running off the road.

[Watch for Wildlife on Road Next 5 mi.]

Frogs.

10:45 p.m.

The rain hits suddenly and hard. Sheets of liquid bullets pound the roof and windshield. The wipers work in vain. This is intense. I can't see. I'm a little scared.

It's just rain.

And the distinct possibility of death.

The sheets of rain turn to torrents, and the fear turns to dread. I slow to a speed I feel wouldn't kill me if I missed a curve in the road. I loosen my death grip on the wheel just enough to not tear it from the console. My back aches. Head hurts.

At a crawling speed, the mesmerizing rhythm of the downpour lets my body handle survival while my brain strikes lightning in rapid and random places, lighting memories of rain.

As a kid, I used to run out joyfully and play in it. Mom would make me come in and say something about lightning being dangerous. I didn't understand. I'd sulk on the couch looking out the front window, wishing I were out there. One day, lightning struck our telephone pole and made our electricity go out. There was a family of fried birds on the ground the next day. I didn't dance in the rain after that, but I still blamed my mom for stealing the fun.

There were many nights as I grew up that I'd breathe deep and doze off to a long, rhythmic lullaby sung by the rain from a spring warm front.

I fight that sleepiness as I drive to the steady, wet rhythm and try to grip that relaxed peace instead of the wheel and the fear.

I listen. Hard. If I listen hard enough . . .

My mind transports to the last time I drove

in a heavy rain like this. I was driving by myself for the first time to Grandpa's house. I was going to spend the weekend with him. We had so much planned, but the storm hovered over us. He smiled in response to every disappointed gesture. With wisdom in his eyes, instead of sharing it, he just offered to play a game or pop popcorn and watch a movie. He loved old Westerns.

A raindrop hits my arm. I look up for a leak and realize it was me.

I haven't cried since before he told us he was dying. I didn't talk to him much after that. Skipped my weekends with him to hang out with my girlfriend. I didn't let him know I got his letters, even though they meant the world to me. When Dad called and told me to meet everyone at the hospital, I went to my friend's instead and distracted myself.

I'm so sorry, Grandpa.

Water pummels the car.

I showed up after you were already gone, just like I hoped. I couldn't handle it. I walked in the room, and everyone was crying. Mom was hysterical and yelled at me. I was cold. Numb. You were just lying there, dead. You looked like a skeleton with skin. Your head was tilted back and mouth wide open.

Aunt Jane put her hand on me and whispered, "After Grandpa took his last breath, a breeze came through the room."

A nurse shuffled in and asked if we could leave and wait in the lobby. I stayed in the corner, letting everyone else go first. I gazed into your milky eyes one last time, looking for you. You weren't there. I don't know why, but I took your journal from the nightstand by your bed. The one you always wrote in on the porch when I came out for morning coffee. The one you opened when we watched a movie I knew you wouldn't be interested in. I slipped it into my backpack and followed the last one out so everyone else in the waiting room could watch us fall apart. I wasn't going to fall apart.

"GOOD GOD, GRANDPA! I WASN'T GOING TO FALL APART!"

I fall apart. Tears flow as I drive through the breaking sky. Heaving sobs unleash uncontrollably as I navigate blind through the dark. The sorrow and guilt at the core of my existence come out as pain-filled screams.

This continues for miles until I feel like a skeleton with skin. How am I still on the road?

The falling flood subsides into an ebbing and almost gentle rain.

12:00 a.m.

I pull into the parking lot of a Motel 6 and consider sleeping in the car so I don't have to move. But it feels like the car is still driving. I grab my backpack and get out to make the illusion of movement settle. I check in for the night, and my body carries me to the elevator to be lifted to my room and hugged by a soft bed.

As I lie flat on top of the tightly tucked sheets, the illusion of forward motion makes me feel like I am rising from the bed, floating. My body is tingling, humming. My mind is grasping for sensory data in the quiet, lightless room. My soul feels empty, but in a good way. Like how you feel better after throwing up. I feel for the remote for the big flat-screen TV and turn it on. Mindlessly, I flip through the channels.

An hour passes. That didn't help. It's all just noise and distraction.

I turn on the bedside lamp and pull open drawers to find out if it's true that there's a Bible in every hotel room. There is. A small, thick, black, hardbound copy with gold inscription: Holy Bible.

If God really has been speaking to me through the scenery, signs, and people so far, then surely He'll speak through His very own Bible. I hold it, closed, binding in my lap, and thumb to the first page that it splits open to.

Leviticus 24:2. "Command the sons of Israel that they bring to you clear oil from beaten olives for the light, to make a lamp burn continually."

Huh? Try again.

Psalm 55:4–6. "My heart is in anguish within me, and the terrors of death have fallen upon me.

Fear and trembling come upon me, and horror has overwhelmed me. I said, 'Oh, that I had wings like a dove! I would fly away and be at rest.'"

That one I can relate to. One more time.

Isaiah 37:38. "Then it came about, as he was worshiping in the house of Nisroch his god, that Adrammelech and Sharezer killed him with the sword; and they escaped into the land of Ararat. And his son Esarhaddon became king in his place."

How do people understand this stuff?

I lay back and close my eyes. It still feels like I'm floating. Floating in black nothing. There is no up. No down. No east or west. Homing in on a high-pitched humming, a car builds itself around me, still floating in the black expanse. Implied purpose, but none in practice. A road unrolls beneath me, stretching to a pointless forever in front of and behind me. There is a familiar rumble of wheels on the road. A large rock comes into view below me, getting larger as it approaches. The road pastes itself to the featureless rock. I now have an up and down but can't tell which direction I'm driving. A light rises in the east, and a wind tears dust from the rock and piles it in dunes. Clouds condense, flash light, and drop water to the ground, making quick canyons and alluvial fans. I drive, looking for Montana as the bare earth builds up and erodes.

The stark absence of grass, trees, cows, birds, and towns—something about it terrifies me and pushes me out of the dream. I sit up, wide awake. I take a few deep breaths and look around. My eyes have adjusted to the low light. I reach for my backpack and pull out my granddad's journal. I look at the last entry. It's dated just a few days ago.

> *I once wrote songs with keen delight,*
> *am now by sorrow driven;*
> *forced to form into melancholy measures.*
> *Wounded Muses dictate what I must write,*
> *Elegiac verses bathe my face with real tears.*
> *Not even terror could overcome from these proceedings,*
> *Faithful companions of my long journey.*
> *Once the glory of my happy and green youth,*

They now console my gloomy fate of age.
For hurried age has come with evils,
And sorrow has ordered her time within
From the head of seasoned gray
To slack skin trembling on exhaustion.

Oh, Boethius. There is no consolation in philosophy,
but you were worthwhile. The soul cannot be contained.

Who is Boethius? Grandpa's writing is fragile yet firm, written lightly but with artistic smoothness. I reread the poem, then begin browsing backward through the rest of the book.

It is one thing to know we are the grass of the field,
quite another to be it.

Am I violating Grandpa's privacy by reading his journal? He never shared it but always had it, frequently stealing moments to jot thoughts on the blank page.

*To see your life from the end. It's not being
here that bothers me, it's all those moments
I lived for what was not real, not honest,
or of no value. I think of all the moments
I was too lazy to write my children and
grandchildren letters. I think of the time I
sold for money, money I spent on squander.
The times I hated taught me life. The times
I loved, I lavished dearly. Of the many paths
I could have taken, could I have made the
train into a station?*

*To see your life from the end is much differ-
ent than to see it from the present, until the
end is near. The immediacy of life demands
both hands. We don't understand the shifting
shade in the sand. Not just to see life from
the end, I wish for my children and grandchildren to live it from the end, to be drawn
into a grand fulfillment of dreams realized,
deep love, and—*

"I'm so sorry, Grandpa." I speak it out loud, as if he can hear me. "For everything. For pulling away when I should have clung close. For not saying goodbye because I couldn't handle it. For being selfish and dishonest. I feel worthless. I love you. I'm sorry."

Speaking the thoughts somehow made what was only in my head before real. The apology and sorrow were real. And with them, a weight lifts, and sleep invites me.

"Good night, Grandpa."

I slip into a deep and restful sleep.

CHAPTER 7

SATURDAY MORNING: SOMEWHERE IN NEBRASKA

6:30 a.m.

Iwake up refreshed. Determined. Alive. The knot in my stomach is gone. My back doesn't ache. I'm up for a drive. If I head back now, I can be home by midnight. The funeral is at four. I can make it to the corner of Montana in a few hours, find a rock, and turn around. I'm so close, and as clear as some things have become, there is still a thick fog in my mind that I feel I have to get through.

6:45 a.m.

I drop off the key at the register and pour myself a cup of complimentary coffee. The automatic doors open, and a blast of unexpectedly cold air opens my eyes wide. A thick fog has covered the land. The ground is reflective. I try to be, but the boost of energy I had waking up is fading fast. I pull out my keys and walk past a man in a coat who gives me a look like I'm crazy in short sleeves. I nod in agreement and walk to the car.

Driving out of the parking lot up to the highway, I've lost my bearings. Which way did I come from? I close my eyes and picture myself in the car, on the road, and driving through the rain. I turned right into the motel. I turn right to continue on. The highway comes to a quick stop at the edge of town. Walmart, gas stations, McDonald's, Taco John's (The Fresh Taste of West-Mex). No Taco Bell, but Taco *John's*? Not even "Taco Juan's." How interesting.

I follow the sign that points toward Hot Springs and take a long gulp from my rapidly cooling coffee.

The mist is so dense I can't tell if I'm in the mountains or not, just that there are lush green hills to both sides—as if rain is no stranger. The leftover rain from last night rests in cool puddles and in ponds on and beside the road.

Leftover rain . . . that's how I feel.

Surrounded by a cloud of witnesses. I've heard that before somewhere. Today, the clouds themselves are the witnesses, and I'm awake enough to know I'm somehow connected. Asleep enough to not know how.

The fog lifts slightly, revealing a picturesque land that doesn't seem to understand its own beauty. In all directions, you could take a picture and sell it on a puzzle. Except locals would look at it and ask why their front yard was so special. Even the occasional abandoned old truck rusting in the field looks like it was placed there for artistic value.

Each time the landscape has changed along the way, it has seemed more and more beautiful. How many times can I be surprised at a view I have never imagined? Is that what art is? If I take the same trip next year, will I be as captivated? I used to enjoy going to the Modern in Fort Worth, but the more times I went, the less interested I was. The last time I went, I just sat at the base of that Jacob's Ladder thing while my friends walked around.

"Listen."

It was my own voice in my own head, but I didn't think it. It was more like the chirps of those birds that seem to come from inside the car. I wouldn't have taken notice, except that it wasn't the first time that word has quieted my musings with the scenery.

Cows are spread out in the field. I guess huddling is a southern thing.

The grass is all the same height and dark green color. It looks like a layer of moss covering every inch of the hills.

[Buffalo Gap National Grasslands]

A railroad cuts through it. The highway cuts through it. Fences and farms. I don't see any buffalo.

It's so hard to listen when there is so much to look at. Trying to listen, I notice how busy my eyes are.

[Welcome to South Dakota]

[Think! Drive Safely]

"Thank you, I will," I say aloud to the sign on the side of the now-widened road.

A faint outline of mountains emerges from the slowly thinning haze. My heart jumps with excitement. My body surges with anticipation.

CHAPTER 8

SATURDAY MORNING: SOUTH DAKOTA

8:00 a.m.

With only a quick hour behind me today, a jagged horizon comes quick. I'm at the mountains! I pass a billboard for Mount Rushmore, the picture right out of the textbooks.

A red barn stands proudly in a green field at the foot of a steep, domineering white cliff. A rusted old metal bridge is out of service, a relic of the days when it was modern.

[Scenic Route]

I see the sign just before I pass it, pointing toward what must be the Black Hills, away from the straight, wide highway ahead of me. I tap the brakes and jerk the car toward what is beautiful.

I'm so used to the phone telling me what to do. I'm going to have to pay better attention to the signs.

I slow down as the road eases between pronounced hills and curves with the land. It's not just a straight, easy path.

I am in awe. White horses graze nonchalantly on tall grass between taller trees midway down an incline, as if they didn't know anything less or more beautiful. Diagonal rock lines explain tectonics on the sides of cliffs close enough on the winding road to touch from the car.

Man is more powerful than the plains but has to submit to the mountains.

[*Crazy Horse* Filmed in This Area]

I watched that movie with my granddad. I can't help but smile.

I drive into Hot Springs, and there is a Taco John's. I have to try it. I order a breakfast burrito and a side of "potato olés." I ask the lady handing out my food if there's a place I could stick my feet in the hot springs for a few minutes.

"Yeah, there's this nice place called Evan's Plunge. It's fed from the spring and has a rock bottom. As you follow the road, it's on the left on the way out of town." It sounds like a great quick stop. I could walk in the warm stream water in the cool air, barefoot on the smooth rocks. Tall trees all around with glimpses of jagged peaks.

I drive through an old downtown that looks like it's still experiencing the good old days that existed only as a memory in those empty towns I passed through in Oklahoma and Kansas. Coffee shops and gift shops fill the buildings, ready for summer traffic.

I see the sign for Evan's Plunge and turn into the parking lot, but all that's here is a faded baby-blue rectangular metal building. This is not what I was expecting. It's just an indoor/outdoor swimming pool and a kids' pool with a few slides. The potato olés were just tater tots. Expectations kill. I continue on my journey.

A few miles out, there's a metal cutout silhouette of a military horse rider planting an American flag on the top of the hill. I remember how *Crazy Horse* ended.

The timber-built frontier houses spaced with acreage look like a dream to live in. Wake up, go to the porch, and sit in the rocking chair as the sun rises. Tourists call the number on your fence for a guided horseback tour of the rugged historical landscape. It sounds nice in my head at first, but I can't seem to shake an uneasiness about the history of conflict, as if it's the same conflict still settling within myself. Something native being taken over.

Settling.

Conflict.

Unsettling.

History and tourism.

I can't dig deep into it. It's like I know there is gold in these thoughts, but I just come up with dirt.

[Large Wildlife on Road]

The shape of an elk on a yellow sign. Mr. Adams would be irked by the lack of an article. I look for large wildlife on the road.

The Black Hills. They aren't really black, and they're much more than hills. Then again, the tall , dark fir trees are such a deep green, they look black in the distance. And they cover the lower-lying hills.

[Buffalo Are Dangerous]

Another warning. I like these signs. Back home, we just have speed limits, exit signs, and "Don't Mess with Texas."

A fair-sized flat field opens up amid the hills. *Whoa! Buffalo!* Right there on the road! There aren't even fences! I slow to a stop way back, not knowing how much danger the warning implies. They stand on the road watching me. Do they have a memory of the land? Are they making a point by standing in the road, not allowing humans to pass?

The strong creatures finally strut off the road, and I cautiously drive by. Little mounds of dirt are scattered across the grassy expanse. Groundhogs? Large, dangerous groundhogs?

Driving through the brief plain and onto a road cut through a curving valley of boulders and evergreens, I distinctly hear the birds again.

I've heard the bird whistles and chirps so many times, I've begun to notice the nuances in their variation. It's rarely just one note. Low to high, high to low. Low high low, low high medium. Some notes are staccato, others slurred together. Clear and crisp. Long with vibrato. I'm surprised I remember some of these terms from middle-school band. In band we just played the songs, and the notes had no meaning other than the pleasure of the sound. We weren't trying to communicate anything. To the birds, this is language. They understand each other.

[Think! Don't Die]

Well, that's a different sign.

The roads wind through jagged rock and frontier hills. The speed limit—55 mph—seems fast around the curves. Not wanting to die, I drive slower and try to take it all in. And think. Friction and inertia help boulders fight gravity. Once friction loses, inertia changes sides. Trees reach upward in worship of their source of life.

Proud of my poetic metaphor . . . I'm not sure it's poetic or a metaphor. And it doesn't work.

Down is not bad; up is not good. Down is down. Up is up. Rocks fall, trees grow. Trees fall, mountains rise. Deep breath. I'm driving through a glimpse of reality with a road running through it, and I don't know what it all means.

There aren't many people on the road, and there haven't been.

Those houses would probably seem large if there weren't rocks twice their size resting next to them. Relativity.

The peaks in the distance are higher than the grass will grow. A few trees try to. Limits.

[Think! Don't Die]

I've seen a few of those signs now. I don't want to die, but I think I'm getting tired of thinking. Even though there is constantly something new to look at, I'm just thinking the same thoughts. The more I think, the more I'm aware of how little I really understand. If God is trying to speak to me, I don't get the meaning. I don't speak bird. I don't speak rock. Maybe it's all for nothing.

Thinking harder won't lead to answers—I don't even know what the questions are.

What does happiness even have to do with anything?

This is dumb. I'm hungry.

9:03 a.m.

Pulling into a town named Custer, I park in front of a T-shirt shop where a worker is filling sale racks on the sidewalk. The shirts all say something related to the Black Hills. Shirts tourists buy to hold on to their memory of a beautiful vacation. I think about buying a fifteen-dollar sweatshirt because it's so cold. But it's May, and I'll be back in Texas soon.

A few shops are open, but the tall brick coffee shop with a larger-than-life John Wayne statue in front has a sign similar to the others: Closed for Winter.

It's May. A few days and another world ago, it was a hundred degrees in Texas!

Across the street is a diner named Baker's Bakery. Their logo is a modest pinup waitress (if a pin-up waitress can be modest) with her skirt blown up in the back. Her hand covers her mouth, and her eyes imply it wasn't intentional. Hamburger buns cover her buns. Unsuspectingly, I walk into the restaurant and stand in line behind a wait-to-be-seated sign. It's a quiet town with closed businesses, similar to the one in Oklahoma. But this place is packed, filled with overhead chatter, clanging from the kitchen, laughter, and life. Part of me is over-whelmed with this reality after so long alone in the car.

At the front of the line now. The waitress shuf-fles tickets by the register hurriedly, looks around frantically, and comes to me in a friendly panic. I notice there are no open tables.

"It's okay," I say. "I can come back. Let these people have the next table."

She graciously tells me it won't be long, but I promise it's not a bother to walk around and come back. It feels good to be kind, and something about this town draws me in.

I walk down a few buildings to a general store, open for the summer. Books, toys, gifts, and candy. Noticing my awkward purposelessness, the woman behind the counter asks if I am looking for anything in particular. She reminds me of my mother.

"I'm just looking." It's all I've been doing. I pick up a book on the struggles between the Natives and settlers of the North American plains and continue wasting time browsing around.

"Don't forget, Mother's Day is tomorrow!" The cashier hollers from across the store.

"Thank you!" Oh. Is there anything I can do or get that would appease my mother now? I'm not sure which would be better, me coming home or just disappearing. I pick up a card anyway and go to the register to pay for the book and Mom's card with her Visa. I recognize how wrong that is and my shoulders droop and my posture fails as I sign the receipt. This isn't the first time I've felt shame, but I think it's the first time I don't have an immediate distraction to push it aside or cover it up.

I sit at an empty table outside Baker's Bakery

and try to think of something to write in the card. A shiver runs through my core as I open the book instead and skim a few chapters. I've heard of Custer's Last Stand. Is that who this town is named after? I don't know a lot about the history, but I know that there were lots of broken treaties and unequal trades for alcohol. There were even some presidents whose policies encouraged the extermination of Natives. The Natives were in the way of progress.

But a lot of what I know is from the Westerns. Grandpa always reminded me there is a little Indian in all of us and a little cowboy too. I wonder if he was talking about more than DNA.

Too cold even for discomfort, I walk back into the diner to the same rush of life and wait in line to be seated. People are in good moods. They seem to know each other. They seem to care about each other. A woman asks a young girl at another table about her softball game. An elderly man flirts with a forty-year-old woman waiting on her to-go order. She doesn't seem to mind; she says maybe they'll get married next week. You don't see this in Dallas. The same waitress comes to me with the same panicked kindness. I'm thinking about just giving up and going home when a deep, boisterous voice saves us both.

"C'mon and take a seat with a few old men." Two chipper old guys are sitting in a booth looking at me with welcoming eyes and joy-filled smiles. One looks like a seasoned sailor with a smooth gray ponytail and healthy goatee. A flat cap covers the other one's equally gray but much shorter hair. He looks like a beat poet.

"Do ya mind?" asks the waitress.

They shake their heads, I shrug, and they motion me over. The one with the ponytail scoots over to give me plenty of room. Trying to ease my obvious unfamiliarity with such interaction, he introduces himself as Tom and his friend as Skip.

I always hate introductions. If I say my name is Red, they look at me funny and say something about me not having red hair. If I say my name is Redemption, they either don't know what to do with it or ask if my parents are religious. But it is what it is.

"My name is Redemption."

Tom starts in first: "From what?"

Then Skip: "Are your parents religious?"

Somehow, today I find comfort in talking to complete strangers about what I usually just shrug off. "I don't know. It seems like a curse to me. I've known quite a few faithless Faiths, hopeless Hopes, and the only girl I know named Chastity, well—"

They laugh like I've told a funny joke. I smile and loosen up a bit.

"Good to meet you, Redemption," Skip says. "Welcome to Baker's Bakery, best food in town."

We make small talk about the beauty of the hills, the schools in Texas, and tourists. I order the first thing on the menu and listen to the old men jabber on about nothing and everything. My plate arrives, and I try to savor every bite without letting the last of it go cold.

"So what brings you to Custer?" Skip inquires.

I want to say I don't know, but that would probably lead to more questions with the same answer. So instead, I announce, "I'm going to Montana."

Skip takes interest. "Which part? Butte is beautiful this time of year."

"You should go see Glacier National Park while there are still glaciers," Tom interjects. "I need to go up there myself. It's been too many years. The last time I went with the family. . ."

I breathe deep with relief at the dodged question. After a few minutes, a question of my own forms itself into words.

"What are the local feelings about Custer?"

"The man or the town?" Skip queries.

"The man the town is named after," I specify.

Tom snorts. "He was an a-hole. In school, we didn't even learn about him. You know, the reason he was so brutal with his war strategy is that he wanted to be president. He felt like the only way he would have a chance was if he had news clippings of sweeping and extravagant war victories against the 'savages.'" He puts air quotes around the word. "He'd kill women and children, armed and unarmed. The more gruesome, the better. It appealed to the voters and special interests of the time."

"How does that make people who live here feel about the name of their home?"

"We don't really think about it," Skip explains. "It's just like in the South you have schools named after Confederate leaders and slave owners. It's just the name of a town."

"Do any Natives live here?"

"A few. But they mainly live in the poorer parts down the hill. They might have a different view of it."

"Is there much tension between Whites and Natives?"

Skip continues with the answers. "Back in the seventies, there was a lot of racial tension all over the country. Around the time of Wounded Knee, there was a Native who was killed, and the White kid got off. They tried to burn down the courthouse and some of the local businesses."

"They didn't get much sympathy back then," Tom adds.

"How is it now?"

Skip says he's a retired teacher. "The kids grow up in school together, play sports with and against each other. There are few racists for sure, a few old hippies, but most are just good people."

"There's probably some class envy," Tom says.

"What do you mean?"

"Well, we're living the good life while they have all the hardships of poverty."

"What is the good life? Does it really depend on income?" I ask.

Tom finds a chance to bring it back to my name. "Well, today it started out as breakfast with a senile friend, and it's ended up with redemption!" They laugh.

I continue with the strands of thought that have been threading through my mind as I drove up the plains. "It feels like the outward battle between the Native and settler represents a battle that goes on inside each of us."

Tom looks at me inquisitively. "You mean like good and evil?"

"No. Something else." I hesitate. "It's not as simple as good and bad."

"Like civilized and uncivilized?" Skip says.

Tom nods. "Or nature and order?"

"Yeah. Along those lines." I wait, hoping they'll keep trying to put it into words for me.

Tom looks at me like he appreciates the thought. "Looks like you've got something to ponder for the road."

"Speaking of thinking on the road," I ask as I get up, "what's with the signs that say 'Think. Don't Die'?"

"Oh, yeah." Tom laughs. "Those mark where idiots died."

My expression must be comical because Skip hurries to explain. "Mostly from texting or drinking and driving. We see a lot of death on this road."

I thank them both for the shared space and conversation, and they return the gratitude and wish me well.

"Don't die!" Tom hollers after me as I pay out and wave goodbye. By the time I reach the door, they've already resumed the wild conversation they were having before opening their moment to me.

Pulling out and away, I catch a glimpse of the water tower on the north side of town. Custer Wildcats, it announces with pride.

10:15 a.m.

[Crazy Horse Trail]

A car is pulled to the side of the road, and four people are outside, looking east with their cell phones out, taking pictures. Following their line of sight, I see a large, hard, stone face protruding from the mountain. Crazy Horse.

He is almost scowling and completely serious as he stoically gazes back over the hills toward Custer. Underneath and around the monumental face, the rock has been slowly and carefully shaved away, insinuating forms not yet revealed. Striations tilt upward in contrast to the bulldozed and dynamited ramp that wraps around the incomplete sculpture. Behind the head, the natural rock formation looks like any other, with shrubs and trees taking root in the crevices. But from forehead to chin and ear to ear, the face is menacingly detailed and complete.

Half rugged, untouched mountain; half intent, conscious construction. It's going to be a long while before Crazy Horse is finished. I wonder how long it took to get him this far. Is the person who started it going to get to see it completed?

My art teacher once gave us a block of clay and some tools. She told us there was a sculpture inside the block, and it was up to us to carve away everything that was not the sculpture. Slowly and carefully, I sliced the clay like delicate cheese until all that was left was a pile of soft clay shavings.

"There wasn't a sculpture in mine," I told her.

She took my tray of shavings and placed them in the kiln. It ended up looking pretty cool.

"Your whole block was art, Red. It just needed to be set free."

I gaze at Crazy Horse finding his slow way out of the rock and try to remember his story. I think about what Skip said. Civilized versus uncivilized. Unrefined versus refined? No. Natural versus unnatural? Native. Native versus what? What is it that I am? What is it that I was born in and raised in? City. Distracted. Busy. Crowded.

As I pull away, I notice a sign for a Boy Scout camp. Somehow, I think it's all related. My block of clay. The peeking face and hidden body of Crazy Horse. History. Scout camp. Paved highway and helicopter tourism. Simple vs. complex?

10:45 a.m.

[Mount Rushmore Next Right]

Stoplight.

Rushmore? Oh, man! I want to stop and see it in real life. I didn't even know it was here. I really didn't even know what or where the Black Hills were either. I wonder how far it is. No, I don't have the time. I've lost enough time here.

The light turns green, and I accelerate forward.

What other faces are hidden in these mountains? What greatness must be done for them to be revealed? What greatness deserves it? Killing Natives? Those who died? The one that figures out the meaning of the relationship between them?

[Hill City]

Unlike Custer, which was still stretching and yawning from a long winter, this town is bustling with tourists. What's the difference? I become more aware of time the slower I have to go. I'm annoyed by people in Black Hills sweatshirts, carelessly crossing the road to the next shop.

I speed back up and enter wooded curves and inclines. Yellow lights flash on a sign with a picture of sheep with big horns.

[Bighorn Sheep: Be Prepared to Stop]

Little birds like chickadees hop around the road, dodging the car, refusing to stare me down like the vulture in Oklahoma. Why aren't there signs that say [Vultures. Be Prepared to Stop]? There were no signs in Hill City that said [Humans. Be Prepared to Stop].

10:40 a.m.

I still can't tell if it's clouds or mist, but it lingers. In my head and above the trees, hinting at the possibility of lifting. It's cold. Isn't that a line from *Catch-22*? When one of the guys is dying? Mr. Adams talked about the warmth of life and something about the soul and coming to terms with when the soul leaves the body, it's just matter. I remember thinking, "What matters isn't matter. What's matter doesn't matter."

A heavy stream of water flows beside the road, winding with my stream of consciousness. High cliffs and tall trees.

[Think! Don't Die]

Colors, water, trees, birds, life. Rock. I want to stop at every pass and take pictures. Even if I could, what is a picture? A snapshot. A visual monument to remember. Would I just remember the place, or would I remember the feeling too? The fog? The sheer beauty. To remember how beautiful nature can be when I go back to the city. To remind me there's a world out here after I get sucked back in. What am I going to do with life?

[Caution: Smoke Ahead]

I look out for bighorn sheep as I see another

flashing sign.

[Be Prepared to Stop]

Either they've learned, or we have.

[Think! Drive Safely]

Vultures circle a close valley. I turn on the heater.

Cliffs of rock were dynamited to make this low curved highway. Neck-tilting trees stretch on either side. It's not the wide-open sky of the plains.

[Caverns]

Caverns. Rock sculpted from the inside by underground water. Negative space. To be defined by your surroundings. To be defined by what you are not. To be something because of something else. To not be something and be something because of it.

[Big Horn Sheep Crossing]

Ravines. Curves. Sheer beauty. The cruise control is on 55, but my foot hovers above the brake.

[Sharp Curves Ahead]

[Fire Danger: Moderate]

[Smokey Bear Prevents Wildfires]

There seems to be an increasing number of warning signs. But what do they mean?!

Around a steep and tight curve, a large body of water reflects the gray sky. Pactola Lake. I pull into an empty parking space at the scenic overview, stretch my legs, and loosen my hands. A fisherman in a small metal boat casts along the opposite shore from where I stand. Without knowing anything about him, I want to be him.

A smooth, round boulder juts out of the water. It's big enough for half a dozen people to stand on, but small enough to be a strange place to plant a flag. Yet the Stars and Stripes flaps in the breeze, reminding drivers, fishers, and tourists alike that even rocks in the water have been conquered and claimed.

11:00 a.m.

Back on the road, the beauty remains. Am I getting used to it? Maybe it's the turns. Unease.

My stomach is tight, head haze remains, and thoughts hit stone walls in search of the sky. I can't see the forest for the trees. What am I doing? I should have just stayed home. I didn't expect it would take this long. I didn't know how long *long* would be.

"Listen."

Ugh. A cavernous yawn reminds me to breathe. I turn down the heater and open the window to welcome some cold.

[Experimental Forest]

What does that even mean?

[Think! Don't Die]

Don't think. Die.

[Damage to Ditch Caused by ATV Punishable]

With an overload of different repeating warning signs, I start imagining "punishable by death" added on to all the signs.

[Bighorn Sheep: Be Prepared to Stop. Punishable by Death]

[Buffalo Are Dangerous. Punishable by Death]

[Damage to Ditch by ATV Punishable by Death]

[Watch Speed. Punishable by Death]

[No Passing Zone. Punishable by Death]

[Don't Go Outside in Lightning. Punishable by Death]

[Watch for Turning Vehicles. Punishable by Death]

[Custer Pass] [Custer Peak] [Custer Road]

The tightness has loosened into a longing. The longing is disgusted by the immediate and opulent appearance of tourist attractions. B&B, Restaurant, Beer, ATV Rentals, T-shirts, Game Ranch, Pioneer-Style Home Rentals, Golf Course, Trout Fishing. The trout fishing sounds exotic, but it's just four rectangular, man-made ponds with wooden piers reaching out into them. Like shooting trout in a barrel. I bet the tourists who signed up for that on their online tourist package expected to be on a raft in a river. Expectations.

There's that old story of the guy on an odyssey, where he is on a journey and gets stuck in a place where it's all nice and relaxing and he never wants to go on. That's what it feels like this part of the Black Hills is for other people . . . but that's not the odyssey I'm on.

[Bear Butte]

I chuckle.

Almost all the houses and buildings are made to look like they did in the past. Even the gas station is made to look like a log cabin. Unlike El Tipi, this one is full of cars being filled and people coming and going.

[Runaway Truck Ramp ½ Mile]

11:33 a.m.

[Deadwood]

Another old Western I watched with Grandpa. Gunslingers and sheriffs. Saloons and gambling. Civilization versus Indians. This town is the most modern I've come across in a while. Shiny plastic signs and fresh construction surround anticipated developments. Large billboards brag about the new casinos and "Old West attitude." The road becomes narrow and congested.

[Detour]

Dead wood grows.

Finally, the twenty-minute crawling detour spits me out north on a four-lane road climbing up and around a domed mountain shoulder.

[Why Die?]

That one didn't even say "Think!" That sign

must belong to a soul like mine, driven to distraction by the mind looking for signs at the right place at the wrong time. His car would have flown from the bend and somersaulted to the tree line.

The wrong way to see the forest . . . from the trees.

[7% Grade]

Is that the grade God has given me on figuring anything out? About right.

[Brake Check]

Brakes work.

[Think!]

Don't think.

[Falling Rock]

[Think!]

Colored rock erodes. Tan, brown, purple, red.

[Think!]

[Think!]

Two deaths in the same spot?

I steal glimpses to my left of the dangerous forested beauty between blinks and through the curves at the base of cliffs. The "Think!" signs may be speaking to those drinking or texting and driving, but if they've been drinking, it's too late to think. If they are texting, they will probably miss the sign. Thinking has almost killed me a few times so far.

[*Focus*] [*Shhh*] Those would do. Thinking and paying attention at the same time is difficult. Thinking feels strangely new to me. This trip is the first time I've really paid attention to my thoughts. It's not like I understand anything, but thinking seems to be something you have to practice to get good at.

I'm about to graduate from high school, and I'm brand new to it.

11:52 a.m.

Out from a long declining thicket of trees, the sky opens up and the land flattens out. That was unexpected. With the same excitement I had when I drove into the Black Hills, I find myself equally excited to be back in the wide familiarity of the sky and straight paths. My hands loosen with the broadened perspective. On to the mountains of Montana. I'm almost there.

Two bird chirps overlap with a brief delay. I'm sure I hear them, but I'm still not sure if they are real. I look around, but there is no bird tree or fence in sight within range of a chirp. Maybe there's a bird in my trunk, experiencing the trip with me, trying to find his song in the meaning of it all. But he's not distracted by the view or trying to come up with metaphors for everything. He's not having to focus on the road.

As I look far into the open sky for the mountains I am chasing, the distant hills still submit to the haze, but the sun seems brighter through it.

I turn onto I-90 West, and a rush of fuel pumps through my veins as I get to push the accelerator to 75.

Ah, speed.

Oh, construction.

I slow back to 55 and watch excavators take red dirt from the raised earth beside the road and place it directly in the dozer's path to widen the existing highway. I never thought about where the materials come from to build the offices, prisons, schools, and overpasses always being constructed in the city. It must be nice to have what you need right where you are. Or to need what you have.

Not quite sure where I'm going, I exit north again toward Belle Fourche. With even just a little distance from the Black Hills, I can tell they impacted me. I was supposed to turn around. I probably should have. Something kept me going.

Beauty. Warning signs. Bare rock. The tension between Native history and conquest in the culture of advancement. Chirp. Fog. Thought. Narrow sky. Nature tourism. Gunfights and gambling.

It all seems connected, but in a way that will only make sense if I stop trying to connect it. Like, if I think about it anymore, a falling rock will hit me or I'll fly off a cliff. I take a deep breath and roll down the window to clear my mind and reset my senses. A bus-sized boulder sits nose first in an otherwise expansively flat field. It just missed me. By a hundred feet and a few thousand years.

Windows down, the breeze is refreshing.

12:15 p.m.

Driving into Belle Fourche, a normal-looking town with people and houses and playgrounds, my body is relaxed and mind paused. An unobtrusive, cool-blue billboard states simply, "Refreshing. 97.9 the Breeze."

I stop to get gas at a station on the corner of the intersection that will lead me to Montana. As I'm filling up the tank, I open the trunk just to see what's inside. Cars don't come with spares? What's a jack without a spare?

There is no bird.

Inside, I walk past the energy drinks and pick up a case of water, some new earplugs, a tire gauge, and a pair of cheap sunglasses.

Back in the car, I feel close. Almost awake. Almost alive. I put on my sunglasses and accelerate west on Highway 212. Almost there.

12:31 p.m.

The two-lane road is rough and loud driving through the green and under the gray. It's too thin to be fog, too thick to be haze. It doesn't look like rain. Smoke from a distant fire? I roll down the window. There's no smoky smell.

The sun getting brighter was just a tease. Or a hint of what's to come? Or a metaphor? I take off the glasses. Whatever it is, the haze still covers the otherwise peaceful scenery, hiding the promise of Montana. Railroad tracks advance on a long, raised mound parallel with the straight two-lane road. I picture kids from the past peering out the train windows, looking for the promise of the West— manifest destiny.

Power lines and fenced hilly plains. No billboards. No thoughts.

12:42 p.m.

How close am I? I picture the mountains appearing from the clouds as soon as I cross into Montana, as if from nowhere—clarity as soon as I get there. For now I'm driving on the treadmill of in between.

Anxiety tenses in my head as an unprompted doubt loosens the muscles in my back and arms. Like my body just gave up.

Little thoughts I've already thought pop up and fade away.

Quiet.

Senses sedated to searching the scenery for spiritual symmetry. I'm on the letter *s* in a word game. *Sky*. Doesn't count if I can't see it. Has it only been twenty minutes? I'm tired.

Remembering the word "refreshing" from the billboard in Belle Fourche, I turn on the radio and find 97.9. Fingers on a piano make fluid chords and slow runs of the scale in melody as a soft tap of a hi-hat keeps the pace uplifted without being jazzy. The piano has always had a way of melting my heart. A woman with the voice of an angel lets out words as if they were being set free from her heart.

"This mountain that's in front of me will be thrown into the midst of the sea." Is that where I am? Is that what happened to the mountains?

"Through it all, my eyes are on You." God? My eyes have been on the road, in the pastures and fields, mountains and hills, forests and lakes—looking for Him. Where has He been? Did I miss Him? Or have my eyes been on Him the whole time?

"Let go my soul and trust in Him. The waves and wind still know His name." *Let go.* The wind. The tops of the grass. The top of my soul.

"It is well"—a crescendo builds—"it is well"—the knot in my stomach rises to my heart with the intensity of the song—"with my soul."

But it's not. I turn off the radio before the hi-hat has another chance to prick me. It is *not* well. I feel like a cavern inside. On a meaningless trip . . . in a meaningless life. Tears roll down my cheeks.

"God, it is not well!" I shout at the windshield. "I don't know what I'm working out or where I'm going! I don't know why I'm here! Why?!"

The car speeds up. My heart races. I grip the wheel. I don't know where I'm headed, but I need to get there fast. My body is angry, rebelling.

Great. Stuck behind a truck kicking up rocks, going 55 in a 70. He pulls over to let me pass, and I floor it.

Chirp, chirp. The bird's tone sounds concerned, pitying. My foot eases on the gas, and I set the cruise. I'm going slow in a world that is going by fast, and my soul just wants to be still. The view is a green, low-growing, flat-but-lumpy variety of lovely.

I'm going to be in trouble. I'm cutting it close with the funeral. Where is Montana? Where are the mountains? Not looking forward to dealing with an upset, yelling parent—

A complex series of chirps interrupts me, as if the bird I can't see is trying to argue with me. Is it even real? Is it just in my head? None of it matters. I just want to find solitude. Be still. Have quiet. Not even the humming of my body.

"But that is your song." The warbling chirp repeats. Goose bumps rise on my forearms. What did I just hear?

Sound of the road.

Hum in my ear.

My song.

CHAPTER 9

SATURDAY AFTERNOON: INTO MONTANA

1:00 p.m.

[Welcome to Montana]

I pull over onto a wide gravel shoulder made for pulling over, in believing disbelief. I made it. I'm finally here! The billboard shows a picture of a river flowing through a deep, colorful rock canyon, snowcapped mountains on the horizon, and plenty of places for happiness to hide. I look around at the great land of Montana around me. Low hills wear a tight blanket of deep green grass, expanding as far as my eyes can see. That's all. That's all? The haze is hiding the mountains, right? I squint to the distance. Where are they? This isn't what I expected. The haze darkens. Or do I?

I drove seventeen hours the first day, eight today, but I could shave off two by taking a different route around the Black Hills, I'm sure. I do the math: 17 + 6 = 23. I could drive an hour in, find my rock, turn around, and still make it back just in time for the funeral. And really, a few minutes late wouldn't be that bad. I'd avoid a screaming lecture before, and maybe the emotions would be different afterward. Death changes people, right?

A twinge of guilt. That was a little selfish. But it's logical. I get back in the car and speed to the limit.

[White Markers Represent Highway Fatalities]

In the middle of the sign is a simple, white cross. I know it's the symbol of Christianity, but I've never understood it. I feel like I should feel guilty for not understanding what it means, but who does? It's something you wear if you're a Christian, but it doesn't mean you're good. Something you put on churches, but it doesn't mean they're actually trying to be like Jesus. It feels like an empty symbol. Like a cavern? It's like the landscapes I've seen on this drive—it might have meant something at first, but the more you see of it, the more it loses meaning and becomes just another blade of grass. Something to mark where someone died. Why? People become a blade of grass. The "Think! Don't Die" signs at least made a little sense. The cross just says "Die."

Earplugs expand and shut out the soft *shhh* of the road. A field of shaved lambs watch me look at them.

1:12 p.m.

It's getting flatter.

Deer lie down off the shoulder as I speed by an expansive field of yellow flowers.

1:32 p.m.

It feels like I'm slowing down.

Are those mountains in the gray horizon?

Where did they go?

1:38 p.m.

Great. Another slow semi. As much as I want to speed by, the ups and downs of the hills are too close together to see oncoming traffic. Riding his tail and feeling the pressure of time, my eyes search past the shoulders for any rock that would do. Just any rock that would be big enough to have happiness under. How big is happiness? Like a snake. A rock big enough for a snake to be under, except not a snake. Happiness. Not a pebble, not a boulder. Any bare spot in the green felt only shows fine tan dirt. My heart is racing. Time is pitted against me. I don't like this feeling. It isn't natural. Or is it? It's telling me something.

Slow down and back off. Calm. Just breathe. Don't let the semi impatience block my vision.

1:44 p.m.

What am I going to do about my girlfriend? Are we making each other better people? No. We're just keeping each other from being lonely. Two half-full people, pouring our fullness back and forth from cup to cup. Right now, I'm empty. And full. How can I explain it when I don't understand myself? All my life has been a reaction, and as the drive has made me silent and alone, I just want to reflect. Not to look at the reflection, but to be it.

Do I break up with her? Try to explain? I can't explain. I can't stay with her. I don't feel like connecting to anyone. My heart speeds up and hands sweat. No man is an island. Why not? Because Mr. Adams said so? I hear a train barreling in the distance but don't even see the tracks. Live my life from the end? Is she who I see at my bedside as I die? No, it's a faceless woman with frail hands holding mine. Life from the end.

I slow down and back off those thoughts. Calm. Just breathe. I don't need to pass those decisions blind.

The road splits a thick grove of trees coming back to life after winter.

Erosion everywhere. Life grows on top and because of it.

The train drums forward. "Manifest destiny" pops into my head again. What does that have to do with it? There is no train. There are no tracks. As I delve into uncharted territory within, I don't need to destroy what is native, develop for the sake of money, kill innocence to win popularity, or set up saloons to distract me as I visit monuments of who and how I was before I got there. I don't need to conquer nature or let nature conquer me, but let erosion shape and provide life, die, and provide life. Or something. I don't know. Truth. Maybe that's what I'm after. Hidden in the haze like the mountains.

Mountains!

Big mountains! Through the haze, along the highway, bare rocks are starting to peek out from the grassy cloak. Scrounging with my eyes, the only bare spots within reach are just white and orange dirt. No rocks. How can there be so much mountain and so little rock?

2:20 p.m.

Oh, time. Oh. I have to turn around.

[Custer National Forest]

But it doesn't feel right. And I've come this far. Whatever this is that has been sneak-attacking me, I am not turning around until I find that rock. Climbing in elevation, I pass more patches of red, tan, and purple—eroded rocks that look like the piles of decorative rocks you buy at Lowe's. I'll know it when I see it. Throwing consequences to the wind, a newfound determination and excitement fills me as I roll down the window and smile.

2:40 p.m.

[Ashland]

The land around Ashland is actually burnt. There must have been a fire in the past few months.

Ash. Land. Burnt. Fertile. I sense meaning. Thoughts resemble sense. Songbirds sing through the earplugs. Flowers bloom. Large wooden crosses hang on houses. They're all similar. Not ornate, but like the ones on the side of the road. Trees sprout new, green growth from their fingers. Another cross on the road. Another cross on a church. Are there really a lot of them, or are they just jumping out to me? They make no sense. Does it really mean something to these people, or do they just wear it on their houses to announce they are Christian?

What does death have to do with it? Are they dead in their homes? Dying in church? I never thought it would bug me so much, not understanding the cross. Is that even a question you can ask a preacher? I know the whole, "Jesus died for our sins" bit, but that doesn't even make sense. It's something you have to say you believe, but *what does it mean*? I don't get it. And how does saying you believe it make you a better person? And why does it feel like a question you're not supposed to ask anyone?

On a strong hill, three large old trees stand next to each other above a forest of saplings. The three big trees resemble the three crosses on the hill in Oklahoma, except instead of being a symbol of death, these trees stand for life. They must have survived threw the fire, the ash a fertile soil for the new generation. In science, I remember learning that the seeds inside pinecones won't grow unless they've been passed through fire.

There is something in the Bible about being baptized by fire. It always sounded a little scary, but there is a lot of me and a lot of the world that I wouldn't mind seeing burned, so long as it meant something new could come from it. Something good.

I ponder the trees, crosses, fires, and seeds a while longer as the scenery blurs by. I feel like I'm onto something, but I'm not able to put words to it. Like there are truths that the soul can know but the mind cannot. But how can I know something if I can't explain it?

Flowers bloom in a field.

Birds soar in the sky.

3:03 p.m.

[Lame Deer]

At first glance, Lame Deer is an impoverished Native town, but not dead or dirty. It's like its name, a creature of nature hurting and tired but not dying. Unable to roam, but no longer hunted. This town is the result of history.

My eyes follow Old Cemetery Road, which is just a short dirt path that leads to a few covered picnic tables. A good place to rest. At the stop sign, there are two wooden signs painted white with stenciled letters: "Our ways are through prayer" and "Help our people; pray for everyone." They look like they have been there for a while. I turn left, off the highway and into town to find the local grocery store.

Not a mile down the road is a building that says "Grocery." The simple brown stucco building has no windows and is decorated only with a few No Loitering signs. Inside it is clean, organized, and full of friendly life. I walk around looking for something easy to eat on the road. Chips and candy don't sound good. Behind the fresh produce aisle is a section of Native American clothes, art, knives, and blankets. I wonder if this is where the local Natives shop for traditional goods, or if it is for tourists traveling through, looking to buy something to show their sensitivity and support for the Natives.

I walk away, even though I am drawn to a sweatshirt with local designs printed on it. It is still cold outside, and I want to support the local economy.

But it's May. And it's my parents' money. How do I support them without buying their culture?

Back around the corner, I grab a bag of carrots and notice a rack of handmade wooden crosses, like the ones on the side of the road. I pick up a cross and look at it. I'll keep it in the car. If I get caught in a daze thinking about mountains, miss a warning sign punishable by death, and roll down a hill, no one will have to buy a cross for my marker.

The cashier is a kid my age, and he jokes about me about having the oddest purchase combination he's ever seen. He wasn't worn down and blank-faced like every other cashier I've ever encountered. Nothing lame about him.

Back outside, a gangster-looking guy leans against the No Loitering sign in front of my car. He looks at me as if he is mentally reciting the entire history of the White man in his land. I awkwardly smile and show him my bag of carrots, proving I'm not just passing through appropriating his culture.

Back to the intersection I turned from, I read the signs again and resume my journey west. "Our ways are through prayer." Were they making a statement to travelers or themselves? "Help our people; pray for everyone." It didn't say, "Help our people, buy our sweatshirts and moccasins." It said, "Help our people; pray for everyone." Everyone in the tribe? Or everyone in the world?

I bite down on a carrot and look over at the cross in the passenger seat. It looks an awful lot like two pieces of wood. An intersection. The letter T. When someone finds me, they might see it and think, "He was a good guy," not knowing how selfish and shallow I can be. Not knowing I've lied and cheated. Not knowing I don't even understand God and have never really asked for forgiveness for anything. I roll down the window and toss out the end of the carrot, not seeing the two Natives walking on the opposite side of the road. Oh, man, I hope it didn't somehow bounce up and hit them. I don't look back to see.

This morning, as I drove out of Nebraska, old trucks became art because of their surroundings. Now the broken trucks, discarded tires, rusted farm equipment, and some of the abandoned houses that spot the increasingly rugged land seem older and more woebegone. But the grandeur of these growing green mountain-hills incorporates them into the greater mosaic. It's an old, old beauty. Each new landscape has been more breathtaking than the last. Will I have any breath left?

A merry-go-round of thoughts bob in and out of my consciousness in tempo with a larger, older song made up of the music of the road, my body's hum, and the wind against the car (with an occasional well-timed *chirp*). Poverty. Natives. The good life. Hope. Inner battle. Wealth. Civilization. Meaninglessness. Despair. War. Prayer.

4:30 p.m.

[Crow Country]

Any relation to the bird I've seen all along the way? If I had my phone, I could search it, but would I? Would I be any better off knowing? What if that connection made everything else make sense? Why are these questions even important? *Are* they important? All these questions I have no answers to. What questions should I ask? Questions are key. Granddad always asked good questions.

Note to future self: ask good questions.

My physics teacher told us the goal of all the science in his field is to come up with a universal theory of everything that is so simple it could fit on a shirt. He was wearing a gray shirt with a yellow smiley face on it. Happiness.

Happiness doesn't explain anything. The universe can't exist just to make me happy, can it? It seems much bigger than that.

Maybe that's what I'm looking for. A theory of everything. All my questions, all the details of the scenery, the birds, the fields, the mountains—they're all connected, and maybe, by answering all the little questions, I can understand the big one. Or if I find the big one, does everything else just fall into place?

Right now, it's all covered in grass. The land is rising and falling, but I get the feeling that even the valleys are getting higher. Like one of those stock-market graphs. Or a heartbeat monitor with the screen tilted slightly upward. That would be a better shirt than the smiley face. With a flat line at the end, a crash.

The landscape is starting to show its long relationship with the cycles of water. Years of rains and runoff fine-tune small canyons and alluvial fans, all still blanketed in green.

I yearn for bare rock.

There is so much surface area, so much land. I feel small.

4:50 p.m.

[Little Bighorn National Monument]

I follow the sign to the gated park and talk with the young park ranger in charge of collecting money. They are about to close.

"You don't have enough time to do the tour and really get how cool it is," he tells me, "but you can still go into the gift shop."

Would that fit on a T-shirt as a summary of the universe? I thank him and turn around.

Back to the highway. Little Bighorn. Oxymoron. Custer meets karma, but the Natives still lose. Paradox? Irony? Coincidence? I get them all confused. If I knew my grammar, would it make more sense? To make sense of something confusing by naming it something confusing makes sense in a confusing sort of way.

5:00 p.m.

The on-ramp to a big highway north makes me focus on the cars going 80 instead of my thoughts at the same speed. Custer didn't make president and went out in a defeat more extravagant than his victories. The man was stopped, but the railways and roads were not. A trucker on my tail makes me grab the wheel tight, glancing back in the rearview until he passes. It takes me a while to figure out the flow of traffic. I've always heard there's no speed limit in Montana.

Finding the safe speed of 82, I breathe deep and feel good. This trip has been a life-changing experience, even though I can't tell you what has changed or why it was important. Maybe it's just that now I know the world is bigger than the city and that the bigger world is not the city. I want to be an old man fishing on a metal boat in a big lake reflecting the sunset. To pull up whatever flag has been placed in my soul, then to explore, conquer, and plant a new one. And to have a wife with frail hands holding mine at the end of a long, worthwhile life.

Even if I had turned around back at the Montana border, it would have been worth it. Should I just call it a victory and go on home? There are no big snowy mountains or rocky cliffs and winding roads. I could go on for days and not feel like I've found what I'm looking for. And still not even know *what* I'm looking for. I don't know how much more driving I can handle. Or how long until enjoying being alone and quiet wears away and I crave the people that, right now, I'm enjoying driving away from.

Does it have anything to do with the prairie dogs on both sides of the road, poking their heads out of their homes in the expanses of dirt? The way they scurry across the highway, not understanding the speed and danger of the passing traffic? Did the one I just hit tell his mom she wouldn't understand as he ran off to find happiness under a clod in Moundtana? They run like they're scared. What are they scared of?

What am I scared of?

The need to find that rock to look under is growing stronger. On a page in Grandpa's journal, I found these words: "yearning, SEHNSUCHT." He'd written them hard and thick, then retraced them. Maybe that's the word for what I'm feeling, even though I don't know what it means. I could just find out what it means. Then would I have meaning?

I won't turn around because I can't turn around. Like the groundhog I hit. There is no home. Just dirt. There is no funeral. Just grass. And crosses. There is an ending that I can't see to or past, but I'm being drawn to it. I'll know where it is when I get there. I'll know what to do when I get there. I'm starting to feel like I'm being led.

The sun peeks through the gray as the fast four-lane highway straightens onto another unexpected flat Montana plain. Plain of thought. Plane of thought. Back pain. Window pane. Turn back? Earth turns. Earth worms. Worm holes. Worn holes. Worn whole.

Birds chirp. Cheap birds. Earplugs. Slug bug.

These roads were made to get people from one place to another as quickly as possible. I've been headed somewhere in a hurry for a long time.

Modern cars to covered wagons. I transition from word games to pretending to be the first to see this land as a pioneer, not knowing where the destination is or what obstacles stand in the way.

Work zone. Slow thoughts. Hungry. Birds speak and wind sings. What does it mean? If I were a character in a book Mr. Adams had me read, wouldn't I argue that everything is meaningless? Living it is different than reading it. Looking for meaning is different than being told meaning. Nature being an expression of something beyond me is beyond me. If nature is the creation of a Creator, and the Creator is unknowable—can we not know at least something about Him by paying attention to that very creation? How can all this have meaning? Am I crazy?

"Listen."

I get quiet.

That dang vulture.

The mirage in the road. The mirage is the road. The road is a mirage?

Humming in the ears.

Sun.

Mist.

Train horn.

It's all overwhelming! It's like when I don't understand what my girlfriend is saying so she just repeats it louder. It doesn't help!

Slow truck. Tight chest. Tight hands. Back off.

Breathe.

Erosion.

Progress.

Signs and warning signs.

Power lines.

Silhouettes. Shadows. Something about Plato, but I don't remember.

Mountains.

Grass.

Cows.

[End Work Zone]

[Speed Limit 80]

[Reduce Speed Ahead]

Reduce speed, head.

5:50 p.m.

Billings seems to be where all the traffic is coming from and going to. The industry is evident from the view of the highway, and there is no sign of mountains and rocks. There is a gas station at the next exit where I can fill up and fill up. Lack of food, lack of gas, and lack of hope all seem to evoke the same feeling.

Food in hand and fuel in the tank, I ask the cashier how close I am to mountains. He's a little older than me, freckled with unkempt red hair. He'd be taller than me if he didn't slouch. "Small mountains or big mountains?"

"The kind that make you happy."

The look on his face shows his confusion. "I don't know. I've been around them all my life." After a moment of searching for a thought behind his blank gaze, he offers with little enthusiasm, "Wanna buy a map?"

I do.

Back in the car, I ravage the curly fries and look at the map for an "X marks the spot" spot. There seems to be topographical suggestions of mountains way far west, but I am starting to expect that expectation kills. I have already failed at imagining how greatly long the Great Plains were, how cautiously tortuous the Black Hills would be, how nonmountainous Montana would be, and just how long this exhausting odyssey will take. The map shows a southern turnoff not far past Billings that would lead me home.

The southward line on the map stares back at me, judging me. "I am the road home from your failed trip," it mocks. "I am the highway of incomplete journeys, almost-realized dreams."

I bet it's a well-worn road.

I take a bite of my seasoned curly fries, take a shallow breath, and slowly accelerate back toward the aggressively fast highway. The seeds of giving up are sown. What am I supposed to expect? Even if I do find the rock?

Cars zoom by. A few honk, annoyed that I'm only going 75.

[Adam and Eve]

It's a billboard of a woman's red lips smirking behind a bitten apple. Eden. Temptation. What is that advertising, and why did it grab my attention so deep?

Before I can give it much more thought, I take a slow curve around a large rockless hill, and I'm left breathless. A gorgeous cliff, cut away by a turning river! Perfect stone debris lies where it landed. Some at the base and some washed by the changing depth of the rushing water. I take the exit and pass under the highway to a parking lot overlooking the mountain slowly trying to work its way to the sea.

I get out of the car and—of course!—the rocks are on the other side of the rapids. I rush to the muddy riverbank, estimating the possibility of wading across the water. I would be swept away. There are no rocks on my side, and I can only admire from afar what I cannot take part in. But I have a taste of food on my tongue, my tank is full, and I have proof that there are rocks in Montana.

Hope.

Back to the car with a few quick steps, I reenter the race, looking to the left and right for the next cutaway. I feel hope in an otherwise unexpectedly unappealing busy city with billboards and unevenly growing trees blocking any suggestion of geographic context. The neon metal palm trees throw me off. A baby bear is dead on the side of the road. I don't know what to expect next.

6:12 p.m.

The word "submit" comes to mind. Relieved it did not require the thought of "think" and the attention of "listen," I say out loud to the bird in the trunk, "Okay."

[Lewis and Clark Trail]

The mist is becoming the remnant of its own memory. I have no pictures to remember this trip by. It was so quick—I'll probably forget everything by the time I'm home. What do pictures even do? Do they really make me remember what it was like, how it felt, or just that I took them? It seems like the moments that call the most for pictures are the moments when I think, "This will be unforgettable."

Then why take a picture if it is unforgettable? To brag? So other people know how cool I am? So it seems like my life is more awesome than it is? I have to admit, there is something that feels good when my friends are jealous of me. But it doesn't feel right. I picture Custer taking pictures of himself for the newspapers in DC.

I'll be okay forgetting every road and thought and site and feeling, so long as I don't forget that there is peace in silence and that through all this time by myself, I've never felt alone. Another swath of rich rock. There is no exit. Fences. It's out of reach.

6:29 p.m.

The sun comes out, glistening on the winding river beside the highway. Where there is water, there are cliffs, there is erosion, there are bridges, birds, trees . . . life. I breathe.

6:37 p.m.

Cliffs, erosion, bridges, birds, trees, and the vulture. My ears are ringing loud.

6:46 p.m.

River. Railroad. Ranches. Dead trees, new growth. Time seems to cover more distance now.

6:56 p.m.

Catching up to the train. Catching up to the terrain. Perfect rocks—on the other side of the fence. Is this where happiness is fenced, herded, milked, and bottled?

[Greycliff]

A bird on the Greycliff sign spreads its tail feathers, showing them off. Getting my attention? Will that be my cliff?

There is no cliff.

[Crazy Mountains]

I expected the Rocky Mountains to be rockier. I won't get my hopes up for "Crazy."

7:07 p.m.

Patience in silence.

Beyond the lifting mist, I didn't believe they were there, but they are! Crazy big mountains! To the distant north, towering peaks are capped in snow. There's a bare area between the white peaks and the mask of grass and trees. A solid gray bedrock in the sky.

The highway is built, logically, in a wide valley. I'm going to have to get off the main road to get to the rocks. But not yet.

Rocks big enough for happiness are here! And there! But the time between seeing perfection and having the time to exit is against me. I'm going too fast, and there are no turnarounds. How do I do this?

"Submit."

Okay.

[Gusty Winds Area]

A gust of wind touches the top of my head as I see the sign.

[Livingstone]

This is it. It's here.

The exit nears, and I slow down with my blinker on. Off the speeding highway, a quiet two-lane road leads me past an abandoned radio station with a deer grazing on the grass growing through the parking lot. On my right, the river flows clear and fast over shallow smooth stones. I feel close. Very close.

But not with excitement and a fast heart.

With a clear and fast peace.

Two small bridges span the running river. After scoping out the first at 30 miles per hour, I brake to turn at the second. I turn right, and just over the bridge is a pebbled shoulder wide enough for a car. I park next to a chain hanging between two knee-high poles.

[Authorized Personnel Only]

The sign is hung from the chain, blocking a path to a rocky riverbank.

My head tells me "here," then head home. But deep inside it feels like settling. And I'm not authorized. Unless God authorized me.

Ding, ding, ding! The railroad crossing lights flash, and arms lower in front of me. A train powers east only a few feet in front of my bumper. I get out and stand to feel the wind on my face. The sound of metal on metal pounds a rhythm like a heartbeat.

Graffiti marks the train cars in neon and black. One catches my eye in legible black and white. "Progress." Progress. The train conquered the West and now carries goods back East. The Native land would disagree with this progress. The buffalo, fenced, don't stand in the way. A kid with spray paint had one word to write. Why this?

The train passes and the steel heartbeat fades. The arms raise on both sides of the tracks, and the clanging crossing bells fall silent. I look past the tracks toward close, humble mountains. Past the farmed valley.

It hits me. *Pro-gress.* The verb, not the noun. I get back in the car and obey, crossing the tracks.

Beyond a small community of clean white houses, a large stone arch announces the entrance to Calvary Cemetery. I breathe deep, look down at the cross in the passenger seat, and progress.

Perfect eroded cliffs sit behind fences. I keep driving around curves and past hilly ranches and small farms.

7:40 p.m.

A few minutes past a few minutes of doubting, a hill cut in half from gravity and erosion protrudes proudly; rocks reflect the late afternoon sun. No fences claim ownership of this sunlit crag.

Off the road and parked in the shade of the stone, I turn off my engine and run around to a climbable slope. My feet guide me to the pinnacle, turning over loose rocks on the way.

I inhale deeply to catch my breath, and there in front of me is a rock so perfect in size and shape, it looks like it was put there on purpose for sitting.

I oblige, accepting the seat and looking out over a view that captures the entirety of my journey.

I can die now.

Cars race on the distant highway here and there. A train progresses alongside the river rapids, which look slow from farther away. Fields, farms, ranches, and woods. The town and the people living town life. The dead find rest at Calvary. Power lines connect houses with electricity through wires on poles the shape of a T.

Lifting my eyes, I behold bare mountains standing like truth above the blanketed mask of the earth and its scenery. Peaks so large that, even in their distance, they testify to the enormity of the solid foundation of the earth as it reaches through to point to the sky. On the rock, my body feels like it is where it is supposed to be—and I'm in it.

A cool breeze comes from the east to the almost setting sun, as if it were going home after a full day of making the tops of fields and minds sway. Geese call from the river. Songbirds serenade from the trees. Fearless prairie dogs peek out, scurry, and play. A heart-shaped cactus is by my left foot and a purple-petaled flower to the right. I stand up firmly on the rock and reach to the sky, stretching beyond the limits of my skin.

Another deep breath and I relax, hop off the rock, look at it, and smile. I give it a good lifting push with my whole body. The opposition forces my shoes into friction with the dirt, and I become the tension between the rock and the ground. It's not a giant rock, but it resists breaking its long relationship with the soil. I give a secondary surge of effort, and the rock loosens and shifts upward. My fingers struggle for a better grip. Initial movement was the hard part, and my muscles release the continued momentum as I feel the weight pivot and gravity pull the rock to rest on its side.

I stand. I look at the patch of dark-brown earth that for so long had been devoid of light and air.

The underneath is now above: happiness. As if God hid it there, in the foothills of one of the least populated and most remote places in the increasingly large nation. Or was it the last retreat of joy? Hiding, waiting for no one to find it. To sustain.

I set it free. Give it to the wind.

In turn, it sets me free, gives me to the wind.

I laugh. All I did was turn over a rock.

I cry. Not the sobbing of sorrow and mourning in the rain, but a life-breathing cry of a grown newborn softly coming into life, seeing everything for the first time, and it being real.

Happiness—like the colors of a painted sky, like coming over a hill with a broad view, or like entering a landscape of previously unimagined artistry. Happiness rises like the dew and dissipates, condenses, and falls—all at the same time.

Something bigger than happiness—glimpses of unveiled reality. Satisfaction and value. All the layers become transparent as I gaze through spring-fed eyes over the scene. I am breathing in more air than I exhale. I am taking in more reflection than I give.

Breath taken. Heart calmed. Eyes cleared. Something in me feels like a city of embers and fire on the edge of a cliff, taken by a rockslide into a high river.

Impulse slides me down from the hill to my passenger door. I grab the cross and dig through my bag for a marker. Lucidity draws me back to the top. I sit on the overturned rock, pull off the marker cap with my mouth, and write my name clearly and with pride. Humbly, I hold the cross with "Redemption" scrawled across the arms, and my focus relaxes peripherally. It all makes sense.

"God. I don't know much about You. I don't read the Bible or pay attention in church. I've been selfish and mean. I've done plenty of things I knew were wrong. But I know, this whole journey, You've been working on me. None of it was meaningless. You've been speaking to me, but I don't know how to listen. You've been showing me, but I don't know how to see. I want to. I believe, but I don't know what to believe. Forgive me. Help me. I'm Yours."

With that prayer, I take the cross and jam it into the ground where the rock once sat. Then I fall to my knees, dead to everything I didn't mean to be. When I rise, it's to the possibility of taking part in a great revealing. With a deep inhale, I feel life enter as the sun exposes all, as if none of it was new. I look down at the cross proclaiming redemption, up to the clarity of the sky, out to the land tracing its history, and around to the mountain taking it all back to bare creation.

Exposed, as a newborn, I search the air for my friend, the vulture. He is not there. The sun is still an hour from setting. I think of the man at the fence in Nebraska. I wait, soaking in how real it all is. It fills my senses. It produces sense. It makes sense.

Grandpa would be proud of me. My kids won't know him but by the stories I tell. Their kids' kids won't know me but by the stories they are told. But something beyond the formalities of names, lineage, and funerals will be told without telling. Deep inside, I know—Grandpa would rather I be here, finding life, than looking over his embalmed body. Starting life from the end. The best respect I can show him is to grow new life from his dead trunk on our family tree.

The vulture! There he is, sensing death to devour, circling above the river and bridges. There were cars at Calvary Cemetery, but he's headed toward me. How powerful and appropriate.

My eyes are focused on the wide-winged savage. The closer he gets, the more I can see of him. Black wings, feathered tips, white head, and tipped tail—wait—that's no vulture! A bald eagle! My jaw drops and hairs raise. I am blown away.

Over my head and on toward the setting sun, the eagle disappears into the details. All the details. They were all on purpose. Mr. Adams was right. I try to add it all up, but it's beyond me. One of my math teachers was overly emphatic at saying, "The sum of the parts is greater than the whole." It didn't make sense in math, but it does now. She also had a poster that said, "You don't have a soul. You *are* a soul. You have a body."

I sit on the overturned rock and watch the sun set over all that was and is, thinking nothing but understanding, feeling empty but feeling full.

8:40 p.m.

With the moment set and settled, I carefully descend from my perspective back to the road. A country couple in a red flatbed pickup pull over and analyze me. "Are you okay?"

"Yeah. I just died."

A little thrown off, the guy in the beard speaks across his silent girl in a bikini. "Okay, just wanted to make sure you weren't in trouble." They sputter off, and a few slow minutes behind, I follow. Birds chirp. Cranes fly overhead. Calvary Cemetery. A train progresses, and I wait at the clanging bells. Everything glows in the twilight. An owl hoots from the top of a tree.

I feel good. I feel new. It's time to rest.

CHAPTER 10

SUNDAY MORNING: LIVINGSTONE, MONTANA

8:12 a.m.

I slept hard in a soft bed in an old hotel at the edge of town. I wake up in a blank page to the sound of steel on the tracks across the street. There is a slight ache in my head from the two days of driving. An internal warmth of comfort comes from not knowing what's next or how I will be.

I walk out into a bright, clear day. No clouds. No mist. The breeze returns from the west, to dance with the living. I turn in the room key and drive slowly with no direction. I'm not quite ready to go. I want to find the river. A crow caws.

9:30 a.m.

Along the river there is a public space with playgrounds, a skate park, walking paths, and mowed fields—all under the presence of the sky-ward mountain peak to the south.

[Sacajawea Park]

At the far reach of the community property and above the flowing water, there are a few wooden park benches amid a blanket of dandelions in different stages of life. No one is there, but I feel welcome.

The clear river runs under a one-lane bridge. Local walkers pause to look over the railing and ponder silently. Rectangular, cut boulders are placed just beyond the dandelions at the riverbank to prevent erosion. Bushes and trees send their roots to the water and branches to the sky, making natural playgrounds for a large community of lively birds. In the river, smoothly rounded pebbles and stones create a low but long island on my side of the bend. A dead tree trunk rests between the rocks and the flow.

The ripples reflect the branches of budding green leaves and the sky. Downward is upward; each direction is heavenward.

The loud and continual *shhh* of the water keeps the highway in the background, in the background. Birds chirp like a soft hi-hat, keeping an uplifting tempo. The song that flows into and out of itself seems eternal. *It is well.*

The sun flashes reflections at the fast, narrow neck of the river before the bridge, contrasted with the dark shadow beneath as the river widens to a calm current. My eye catches a tree branch floating into vision, and I watch it experience the changes in the nature of the water as it progresses around the bend, under the bridge, and out of sight. I wonder if it is paying attention. A dove flits from the bushes and sits with me.

I'm entranced by the river's flow, the visual and audible song, and the lightness of my soul. There may be no such thing as silence, but there is peace in the quietness of the mind. Why was I so afraid of quiet? Why was I so afraid to be alone? It's like the things that filled my ears and eyes, that distracted my mind and heart—they had a grip on me. The TV, phone, computer, radio, girlfriend—they relied on my devoted attention, needed me to need them, and needed me not to change. A lie can only live if it's mistaken for truth. The grass loves to be mistaken for the mountain. The veil loves to be mistaken for the face. I peer over the water at the bare face of what lies beneath also rising above. The breeze tousles my hair.

A stout, determined old man with a long hermit beard and winter cap is walking on the path behind me, carrying a door on his slouched back. I turn my head and watch him curiously as he carries the wooden fixture to the middle of the bridge. He puts it down, leaning it against the railing for a rest. It looks a little like the front door to my granddad's house—aged solid wood with three small windows at the top. My head cocks in surprise as the strong old man shoves the door over the rail and into the river. Without looking over, he walks on. Strange.

The door landed partially on the rock island and does not flow downstream. I look around to see if anyone is there to tell me to stay out of the river. With piqued interest, I climb down the boulders, take off my shoes, and wade to the island of soft pebbles and stones. In the thirty yards or so it takes to walk to the door, I pick up five perfect skipping rocks.

The door is just what it seemed: an antique, solid wood, hand-routered piece of residential history. The handle facing me is not a typical knob but a thin metal lever. The paint is peeling, but not so much that the person who wrote on it couldn't write on it. The entire door is covered in words written in permanent marker. I drag the oddity out of the water.

On the top left corner of the outer side of the door, written in bold capital letters: "ECCLESIASTES." I know it's a book of the Bible because it's the one my Sunday school teacher thought was depressing and told us to avoid if we were just learning about God. Someone has scrawled text from the book on this door. There are no chapters or verses marked, and the writing takes up most of both sides of the door. I skim the words.

The words of the Teacher . . . "Meaningless! Meaningless!" says the Teacher. "Utterly meaningless! Everything is meaningless."

What do people gain from all their labors at which they toil under the sun? Generations come and generations go, but the earth remains forever. The sun rises and the sun sets, and hurries back to where it rises. The wind blows to the south and turns to the north; round and round it goes, ever returning on its course. All streams flow into the sea, yet the sea is never full. To the place the streams come from, there they return again.

All things are wearisome, more than one can say. The eye never has enough of seeing, nor the ear its fill of hearing. What has been done will be done again; there is nothing new under the sun.

I read the whole thing twice, and rather than it being depressing, I find it quite refreshing. With so much being meaningless, it begs the question: what is meaningful? I used to want to be popular. I used to want the prettiest girl. I used to want to be comfortable and distracted. Now, I just want a meaningful life.

It's like the ancient writer was having the same experience as me. Under the same sun, kissed by the same breeze, sitting by the same water. I feel full in our shared smallness as I finish the last sentence again and look up toward the huge universality that we exist in. Both of us, all of us, at all times at once.

It only feels appropriate to push the door off the island and on down the river. It floats away like so many moments beyond perception.

There is still no one on this far end of the park, but I look around anyway. I want to skip some rocks. I didn't see any signs saying "Stay off River. Punishable by Death," but I don't want to draw attention.

A dog dives into the water about the same place I left my shoes. Two boys follow, not taking off their shoes. People arriving. A mother slowly climbs down the black boulders, correcting and warning the boys of the dangers of life and dirtying their clothes. I take this as a go-ahead and launch a few stones, skipping them against the small rapids to see how they react. Each result depends on so much.

The boys, probably a few years apart, dart for the tree trunk as if it were a new addition to their usual playground. I stay at my far end of the isle and skip rocks under the bridge to the smoother waters. My cheeks are sore from smiling.

When my arm can take no more, I pile the smooth rocks on top of each other, making stacks like I have seen in pictures. The wind knocks them down. Childhood laughter and the mother's correction in the background, I smile and do it again. Those kids are happy, too. I remember that. I wish someone had told me to remember what it was like to be a kid when I was still that young.

The moment is fulfilled, and I wade back over to the embankment, grab my shoes, and climb back to my bench. I allow the cool sun to dry my feet before I put my shoes back on, watching as the family dog chases after another dog being walked without a leash. Both owners call their dogs' names, to no avail. The dogs are free. The kids are free.

Mother knows best, and soon playtime is over. She sits on the bench next to me as her children make their way toward her instruction. She sighs a sigh of a mother's exhaustion.

She initiates friendly small talk, giving the boys and dog a little more time to get their energy out.

"Do you ever get used to the beauty?" I ask her.

"No, but we do find ourselves moving every five years or so, and we're only three years in here, so it's still pretty fresh."

As her kids come ashore and climb the rocks, the dog plays with its new friend. The mom gets up and tries to lead their dog back toward the car. The boys don't miss the opportunity to climb a tree.

Dog in hand, the mother looks over at the boys. "C'mon, let's get changed for church. There's no way we're going in mud-covered trousers."

As they finally reach their car, an elderly couple parks and slowly finds each other's arms to walk leisurely among the dandelions.

Church. Maybe I should go.

10:41 a.m.

I zigzag the length of the town from the river, one street at a time. Most of the people I see are either walking for exercise or doing lawn work. I expect to see a church at some point.

There it is.

I turn in front of a redbrick church with a white wooden steeple lifting a cross toward the bright blue sky. Thick, clean white trim frames old stained-glass windows. A simple glass design of a lily on the river in the valley rests above the tall, wooden double doors. To the left of the entrance is a sign with the words "Living Hope Church." The O in *hope* is a sun with a cross on a small cliff partway up the side of a mountain. Below the name are service times and a verse. I stop to read them.

Worship starts at eleven, and the quote is from Psalm 139: "You are beautifully and wonderfully made."

I park down the street and wait for the service to start. I don't need a generic greeting and small talk. I want to see if God will tie up some loose ends. If the songs and the sermon can straighten my question marks.

11:05 a.m.

I wait until the greeter lets the oversized door ease shut behind him, then I enter quietly, pick up a bulletin, and find the back pew. The congregants are already standing and singing. I am suddenly aware of my greasy hair, three-day-old clothes, and forgotten hygiene. I should have showered at the hotel. Oh well. No one seems to notice as they are all singing, "Be thou my vision . . . thy presence my light." A man with a microphone earpiece is playing a Native drum to the music.

There are a few kids my age—one restless, one bored, and one really into it with his eyes closed and arms raised. One of the women singing by the piano reminds me of an older version of a girl I know back home. In fact, a lot of the mothers and fathers look like slightly aged versions of people I go to school with.

The songs sound oddly familiar. One phrase catches my attention: "Blessed redeemer, Emmanuel." What does that even mean? I've been around these words, but it's like a different language. Other phrases in the songs speak directly to me. "I'm alive."

The preacher puts down his drum and stands as the congregation sits. "This week, we'll continue with our study of the book of First John and reflect on the nature and importance of belief." He opens the Bible to First John and reads the entirety of chapter 5.

The building is old, but the carpet is new and soft. The pews show craftsmanship and artistry that must have been done a few generations ago, but the cushions are springy and comfortable. A large cross hangs behind the stage. I picture the word "Redemption" written across it. I run last night through my head again—it made perfect sense in the moment, but now I'm getting confused by the meaning of it all. It's like I have a new life, but I need to learn a new language to make sense of it.

Belief. What do I believe? Before this trip, I thought most religious people were a little nuts. I didn't see much difference between Greek mythology and what I'd learned in Sunday school. And honestly, I didn't think too much about it. I guess I've always assumed there's something bigger than us, and because I grew up around it, I would have told people I was a Christian. But I've never really tried to figure out what I believe. Let's see . . .

I'm fully convinced there is a God. I believe He is trying to talk to us and can use anything to get through. He seems to hear what I've been saying to Him. It's like He wants us to understand, wants us to think, pay attention, and search. I believe He has a purpose in what He does. I feel like I've just started a deeper life than the one I was living, and that's where He wants me. I believe something had to die to get me here. And I believe it because I've experienced it.

They might not all be good ideas that make sense—because they don't—but I've experienced them as true. Would I be able to believe all that if I hadn't actually lived it?

The preacher finishes the Scripture and segues into a blessing poem for mothers. I look down at my program and notice the cover art and theme.

Oh yeah. It's Mother's Day.

He recites the poem, which is careful to include all kinds of mothers. Ones who have lost a child, who have been unable to conceive, single moms, and those celebrating. "To those with teenagers who are lost and frustrated, alienated and afflicted . . . " I have grieved my mother.

At the end of the poem, some men come up and take small potted flowers to hand out to the women in the pews. I ask for one for my mom and study its design.

The preacher guides us through a prayer with long enough pauses for our brains to fill in the silence with our own words. "We confess our sins . . . And thank You for washing us of them and giving us a new tomorrow . . . We lift up this body . . . this community . . . our nation . . . the wars, both internal and external . . . and know that You hear our personal prayers." I take a pencil from the pew and jot notes on my bulletin so I remember how to pray like this. After a long silence, the preacher says "Amen," and our attention follows him back to his drum.

We stand and sing again. I close my eyes and soak it in. "Lightning and thunder . . . living water such a mystery . . . You are the one our hearts always hunger for."

The clock on the wall next to the pulpit is large enough I can see the minute hand moving from the back of the room. The preacher gets up with fifteen minutes until noon. Two of the teenagers and a few adults are eyeing the clock. Why do I care? I'm in no hurry now.

The minister gives a brief background of the book of First John and the chapters already covered with PowerPoint slides projected behind him. I write down all I can fit on the back of my bulletin.

1 John 1—Confidence we have in a historical, flesh-and-blood Jesus. Not a prophet, not a vision, but God in human form.

I don't understand that. I never have. Any time I asked about how Jesus could be God, I was told not to doubt but to believe. Shouldn't we be able to understand what we believe? Would I believe if I'd been there two thousand years ago? If I'd experienced it? Would I be able to explain it to others so they would believe all these years later? Is that what the preacher is trying to do?

1 John 2—Faith is not just about information but about transformation.

1 John 3—We are lavishly loved by God, and He is working out His good will in, for, and through us.

1 John 4—Even in the really hard questions, Jesus reveals Himself to us in the flesh and invites us to live life in Him.

This is going way too fast. The minute hand has hardly moved, but my own hand scribbles to keep up.

1 John 5—Certain faith: "That you may know." Veritas = truth. Can we really know truth? To some lady at Harvard, no. To the author of John, yes.

Then the preacher opens my eyes, gives me goose bumps, and makes my heart stop.

"The word 'truth' that the author keeps using," he says, "translates from Greek to English as the words 'unveiled reality.'"

Like the rock! Like the glimpses of being a part of something much larger, with purpose, with guidance, with life, and with truth!

He summarizes 1 John 5 and leaves me yearning for so much more. Take the clock off the wall. Throw it in the river!

We can know because we can carry out Christ's commands. Falling in love with God's people is falling in love with God because we are in Him. That "in Him"—for the first time after a thousand times hearing it—finally makes sense. The words didn't change, but my ears and my mind have. Let me hear everything else a thousand times until it makes sense!

We can know because of the testimony we have been given. It wasn't by visions or mystics. Three generations after Jesus, they were already asking, did it really happen that way? I have asked the same question. We can know because it is revealed in Scripture. I've never really read it. But if it is all like this, I should.

And just like that, it is over. I want more. I've had a drink, and now I feel how thirsty I am.

Standing with the others for the last song, I grab my plant and quietly leave ahead of the ushers walking toward the door. I have time enough to pause, look at the exit sign, and wonder if they have it backward. Filled with hope, and touched by love, I am reentering the world. I think of the people in the chairs. The kids, the parents who look like my friends in the future. I don't know them, but I love them. I think of the Natives in Lame Deer and say a prayer for them as I walk toward my car. I think of my family, my earliest memories. When did it all start to go downhill? A lot of it was me. I love them.

7:40 p.m.

And now I am back on the bench by the river, writing this all down in my previously empty English journal. Maybe it will help explain it all to Mom. I need to call her. I'll drive to the next town and call from a hotel—let the emotions from the funeral subside a little.

I need to go home. But how will it be? I'm a different person, and I want to grow from this ground I've found at the foot of this mountain. How will it be with my girlfriend? Friends? The city, distractions, old habits? Maybe it will be good to be grounded until I go off to college. Do I still want to go to college in the city? Anxiety.

Back off. Breathe. I let those fast thoughts pass.

"God, I'm Yours now. I'm ready for whatever journey is next. I want to know more. I want to believe in truth. I want to believe truth. I want to keep my eyes on You as You reveal it. Help me to do that. Amen."

I need to take a bath.

* * *

I wish I could say I made it home, that everything started making sense, that my relationship with my parents was healed, and that life became miraculously amazing. A week has passed, and I'm sitting under an overpass in a trainyard in Denver, waiting for the right train to hop home. Recreating it by writing it all down has helped so far.

So far. I've come so far. I've still got a long way to go.

Back to last Sunday.

CHAPTER 11

SUNDAY EVENING: HEADING HOME

8:45 p.m.

The sun is setting, the tank is full, and I am on the road home. The sky is wide and full of color as the land darkens to rest. Peace fills me with each breath.

Slam! An elk rams the front end of my car, and the force lunges me into the punch of the airbag.

I push my way out of the airbag and open the door. I glare at the magnificent beast, and in its eyes, I see the same shock and anger I'm feeling. My adrenaline is pumping. What do I do? The elk huffs mist out of its nose and bolts across the two-lane road into the shadows. What in the world! I want to cuss but clench my jaw shut instead.

The car is totaled. The front passenger tire is flat on the ground, and my hood is crumpled into the engine. What do I do?

I squeeze my hands on my head to stop the pounding.

Shaking my fists to the sky in the middle of the road, I shout at God. "What did I do? Why did You do that? I was going home!"

I'm leaning against the car, trying to stop the spinning, when a motorcyclist pulls up beside me. He leans the bike and puts his feet on the ground. The matte-black helmet turns toward me as he moves his hands from the handlebars to his head. Removing the helmet reveals a strong-faced man with intense eyes, a short, well-groomed beard, and a full head of long, thick hair. With his defined jawline and thick skin, he looks Native, yet he's definitely White. Maybe fifty years old, but marks of wisdom are etched in young wrinkles between his eyebrows and at the corners of his eyes.

Is this Jesus? Was he sent from God?

With an earnest look in his sturdy gaze and a half smile that sees how it is, he asks, "Need a ride?"

"All the way to Texas?"

"I can get you to Denver in a few days."

Not knowing what to do, willing to trust anything, and seeing few options, I give in. "Okay."

"Hop on. People call me Longstoryshort."

EPILOGUE

So you've read this much, and you're probably thinking, "What? How did he get home? How is that the end?" Well, I'm not home yet. It's another long story, and I'm working on that. It takes a lot of concentration to remember the details and try to figure out how everything ties in.

The truth of it is, Longstoryshort was no Jesus. It's like I found God and gave myself over to Him, and immediately things got harder.

You might also be wondering why I published my journal. Maybe it's because I know a lot of other kids my age wouldn't take the journey. Maybe a lot of them would turn back at one of the many opportunities I had—but I want them to live somehow through my experience. Maybe if I share what happened to me, it will make others give thought to the reality of God, to the ways He tries to speak to us, and to our need to be quiet and pay attention.

I don't know; I feel like everybody's got to find it on their own. Plus, I set happiness free. Who knows where it ended up?

To be honest, I think I really published it because Mr. Adams told me once that I don't have a right to criticize a book until I've written one.

Oh, and so you know, part of the proceeds of this book will be donated to the John Woodenlegs Memorial Library of the Northern Cheyenne Tribe (what the people of Lame Deer are a part of). Hey, every little bit counts, right? But if you really want to help them, do what they've asked: pray for everyone.